Robert Dungarran was on the road to London.

Hunting in the mist, rain and snow of Leicestershire had been dismal, and the society there even less attractive. What was more annoying was the meeting with Hester Perceval... How strange that he hadn't recognised her!

When he had first seen her coming round the corner with her cousins she had seemed a different creature altogether. Laughing, animated, capable. It had taken a minute or two to remember what a bore she had been—and the devilishly awkward circumstances of their last meeting... Still, if what she had said about not coming to town for the Season was right, he wouldn't have to see her again... How did Hugo, the most polished of men, come to have such a dull stick for a sister?

Dungarran settled back more comfortably against the squabs and composed himself for sleep. But sleep eluded him. Memories of Hester Perceval flitted about his mind like ghosts.

A young woman disappears.
A husband is suspected of murder.
Stirring times for all the neighbourhood in

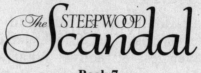

Book 7

When the debauched Marquis of Sywell won
Steepwood Abbey years ago at cards, it led to the death
of the then Earl of Yardley. Now he's caused scandal
again by marrying a girl out of his class—and young
enough to be his granddaughter! After being married
only a short time, the Marchioness has disappeared,
leaving no trace of her whereabouts. There is every
expectation that yet more scandals will emerge, though
no one yet knows just how shocking they will be.

The four villages surrounding the Steepwood Abbey
estate are in turmoil, not only with the dire goings-on
at the Abbey, but also with their own affairs. Each
story in **The Steepwood Scandal** follows the mystery
behind the disappearance of the young woman, and the
individual romances of lovers connected in some way
with the intrigue.

Regency Drama
intrigue, mischief...and marriage

AN UNREASONABLE MATCH

Sylvia Andrew

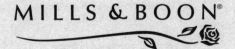
MILLS & BOON®

First published in Great Britain 2001
Harlequin Mills & Boon Limited,
Eton House, 18-24 Paradise Road, Richmond, Surrey TW9 1SR

© Harlequin Books S.A. 2001

Special thanks and acknowledgement are given to Sylvia Andrew
for her contribution to The Steepwood Scandal series.

ISBN 0 263 82848 4

Set in Times Roman 10½ on 12½ pt.
119-1101-63525

Printed and bound in Spain
by Litografia Rosés S.A., Barcelona

Sylvia Andrew taught modern languages for years, ending up as Vice-Principal of a sixth-form college. She lives in Somerset with two cats, a dog, and a husband who has a very necessary sense of humour and a stern approach to punctuation. Sylvia has one daughter living in London, and they share a lively interest in the theatre. She describes herself as an 'unrepentant romantic'.

Look out for
AN INESCAPABLE MATCH
by Sylvia Andrew

in **The Steepwood Scandal**
Coming soon

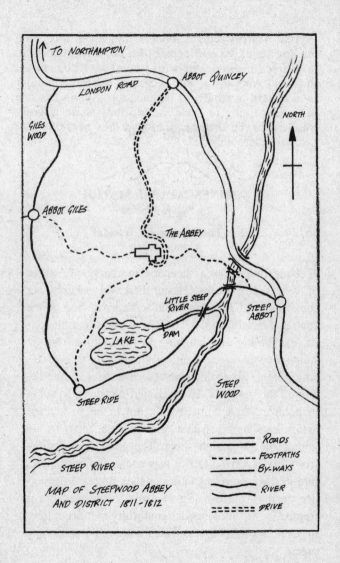

TO NORTHAMPTON

LONDON ROAD

ABBOT QUINCEY

GILES WOOD

NORTH

ABBOT GILES

THE ABBEY

LITTLE STEEP RIVER

STEEP ABBOT

DAM

LAKE

STEEP WOOD

STEEP RIDE

STEEP RIVER

MAP OF STEEPWOOD ABBEY
AND DISTRICT 1811 - 1812

ROADS

FOOTPATHS

BY-WAYS

RIVER

DRIVE

Chapter One

1812

Feeling rather like a sheepdog in charge of a flock of very pretty lambs, Hester Perceval ushered her cousins out of Mr Hammond's draper's shop in the centre of Northampton. They were all in tearing spirits, exclaiming and laughing as they slipped on the snow-covered street, frantically clutching the parcels which they had adamantly refused to leave to be delivered the next day. Even Hester, normally so sober in public, found it impossible not to laugh at their antics, as she helped first one, then the other to negotiate the busy high street. The gentleman coming from the Receiving Office was enchanted by the picture of the four young ladies as they rounded the corner from Abington Street—rosy, animated faces framed in fur-lined hoods, youthfully slender figures in their warm pelisses, blue, wine-red, russet and green.

Just a few yards from the Peacock, Henrietta, the youngest of the cousins, slipped yet again and lost her balance. Hester managed to save her from falling, but dropped her own parcel in the snow as she did so. The gentleman hurried towards them and picked up the sadly sodden package. He held it for a moment, then said with a charming smile, 'I think the damage is superficial. Would you like it, or shall I hand it to the boy at the inn for treatment? I take it that you are making for the Peacock? Your servant is no doubt waiting for you there.'

Hester caught her breath in shock. A deep, drawling voice, a tall, elegant figure. Dungarran. Impossible to forget him, however often she may have wished to. Fortunately, the gentleman had apparently found it perfectly possible to forget her!

'Thank you, sir,' she said, keeping her head down. 'Our groom will be here in a few minutes. He has gone to fetch my brother from the Cambridge coach. We have a parlour bespoke in the Peacock, where we shall wait for him.' She turned to follow her cousins.

'Wait a moment!' He came round and stared hard at her. 'It's Miss Perceval, is it not? Hugo Perceval's sister! Well, well!' He looked at the three girls, standing in amazement behind Hester. 'Are these your sisters?'

'My cousins, Lord Dungarran.'

'But what am I thinking of! You shouldn't stand on the street in this weather. Come! You must allow me to escort you into the inn. We can talk inside.'

Hester hoped that her dislike of the idea did not

show on her face. It was impossible to refuse. He was right to express surprise, however disguised, at the lack of a maid or groom to attend them in such a busy town. It was certainly unheard of in London. And Dungarran, she thought bitterly, was the example *par excellence* of a London gentleman.

Inside the inn the landlord greeted her party with friendly respect. 'The parlour is ready, Miss Perceval, and I've laid out some pasties and pies in case you need something to keep you going. Shall I fetch some coffee or tea? Or would you like a drop of negus? It's cold enough outside, and shopping is thirsty work.'

'Thank you, Mr Watkins.' The innkeeper looked inquiringly at her escort. 'Lord Dungarran will join us until my brother arrives.'

'However, I'd like something stronger than negus, landlord. Have you a pint of good ale?'

'The best, my lord! Please to come this way.' He led them into a cheerful room, furnished with a table and cushioned settles, and warmed by a glowing fire. 'You'll be comfortable in here. We've sent the boy to Hammond's to have your parcel rewrapped, Miss Perceval. He should be back in a moment.'

Hester thanked him and he disappeared. There was slight pause, then she said coolly, 'Girls, I'd like to present a friend of Hugo's. Lord Dungarran, my cousins Miss Edwina Perceval, Miss Frederica and Miss Henrietta.' The girls curtsied rather solemnly. They all regarded their cousin Hugo with some awe, and this friend of his was just as impressive. The greatcoat he had removed on coming into the inn had no fewer than five capes, and one could see now that his indoor clothing—dark blue coat, a snowy, immaculately starched cravat, light-coloured buckskins—was in the first stare of fashion. They gazed at his tall figure and handsome looks, his short black hair and lazy grey eyes, with guarded admiration. However, they relaxed when Lord Dungarran smiled and said, 'I am charmed, ladies. Truly charmed. But I am consumed with curiosity, too. Tell me what is in those intriguing parcels which you are so reluctant to relinquish.'

The girls laughed and put their parcels down on one of the settles. At the same time they loosened their pelisses and took off their hoods. Hester slowly followed suit. Henrietta, the youngest and least shy, said eagerly, 'Muslins and silks. For dresses. We are all to have some new evening dresses, even me. Robina is coming out in the spring.'

Dungarran looked enquiringly at Hester. 'Robina is my eldest cousin,' she said colourlessly, not looking at him. 'She is not with us today. My aunt is taking her to London some time in March for her début in society.' She could feel the colour rising in her cheeks. Her own catastrophic début six years before had been witnessed by the gentleman standing before her. Indeed, he had been a key player and from the conscious look on his face he, too, was aware of awkwardness in the situation. Fortunately for her peace of mind the landlord reappeared with a tray laden with warm drinks and Dungarran's ale. By the time he had removed the covers from the food laid out on the table, adjured them to enjoy it, and gone out again, Hester had recovered her composure. Dungarran cleared his throat.

'Did you say Hugo has been in Cambridge, Miss Perceval? I thought he was in Gloucestershire with the Beaufort?'

'He is. We are meeting my other brother. My younger brother, Lowell. He should be here at any moment.'

Reminded of their favourite's imminent arrival, the girls went to look out of the window. Hester and Dungarran were left by the fire. Hester felt she must break the uncomfortable silence that followed.

'Are you staying in the district?' she asked stiffly. 'Althorp, perhaps?'

'Er…no. I was at my own place in Leicestershire, but the weather hasn't been good for hunting. I've decided to return to London. I've things to do there.'

Hester took a sip of her wine, and turned away to look at the girls. Why didn't Lowell come? It was impossible to sustain a casual conversation with this man. Yet it would be humiliating if he was reminded of the girl she had been six years ago—scornful of small talk, determined to discuss serious matters of state and politics, inept and unskilled in the manners of society… And, for a short while, stupidly in love with him. Her cheeks grew warm with shame and resentment at the memory of their last encounter. How she had hated him after that…!

'I hope the coach is not delayed by the weather. Would you like me to make enquiries?'

Hester pulled herself together and spoke as civilly as she could. 'Thank you, but we were early. It wasn't due before the hour. But please—you mustn't let us delay you. We are quite safe and comfortable here. The landlord is an old friend.'

'So I have observed. Very well, I shall finish my ale, and then be on my way.'

She was hard put to it to disguise her relief. Though the violent emotions of six years before had long been mastered and then forgotten, she still disliked and distrusted this man. She would be glad to see him go. Unfortunately, at that moment Henrietta scrambled from the window-seat and ran to the door, calling Lowell's name. Hester sighed. Dungarran would now be bound to stay a short while longer.

'But I think I know your brother already, Miss Perceval,' he said when she had introduced them. He turned to Lowell. 'I've seen you at White's with Hugo, but we didn't have an opportunity to speak. But tell me, are you still up at Cambridge?'

Lowell flushed with pleasure at this evidence that the great man had taken notice of him. 'No, I came down some time ago,' he replied. 'But I still have friends there. In fact I've just been arranging to share rooms with one of them when he comes to London in the spring. At the moment I'm living at Hugo's lodgings when I'm in town.'

'Why haven't we met more often?'

'Oh, Hugo's mode of life is a touch above mine, Lord Dungarran. We each go our own way.'

Dungarran nodded. 'All the same, we must meet again in London.'

In spite of her unease, Hester was amused at her brother's efforts to imitate the elegance of Dungarran's manner—Lowell was normally loudly self-confident, boisterous even. It was proof, if any were needed, of Dungarran's status in the closed world of London society. But the next moment she was horrified to hear her brother say somewhat shyly, 'Are you staying long in Northampton, sir? I am sure my family would be pleased to receive you at Abbot Quincey.'

She breathed again when she heard Dungarran expressing regret that he had to be on his way. 'I merely called in at the Receiving Office here. I had some enquiries to make. Miss Perceval, it was a pleasure to meet you again. Will you be joining your cousin in London for the Season?'

This harmless question roused a storm of protest in Hester's breast but she replied calmly. 'I am not sure, but I doubt it, Lord Dungarran. There's…there's always so much to occupy me at Abbot Quincey.' Then, she could not help adding, 'I'm sure you will be kind to Robina—she is very young.'

He gave her a sharp look then bowed, took smiling leave of the rest and left. Hester breathed a huge sigh of relief and prepared to gather her party together for the journey home.

Later, after they had deposited the three girls at the Vicarage in Abbot Quincey and were rolling up the drive to Perceval Hall, Lowell said, 'He's a great chap, Hester.'

'Please, Lowell, can we now leave the subject of Dungarran! Ever since we left Northampton the girls have talked of nothing but the polish of his address, the attraction of his looks, the elegance of his clothes, till I was sick of hearing his name. Surely there are more interesting topics of conversation?'

Lowell looked curiously at her. 'Come, it wasn't as bad as all that. I thought they talked quite as much about their shopping, and the dresses they were having made. What's wrong, Hes?'

Hester could not reply. The unexpected encounter with Dungarran had stirred up feelings she thought she had conquered years before. Anger and humiliation were choking her, six years' peaceful reconstruction of her pride and confidence were momentarily forgotten. Lowell waited patiently. He and Hester were very close. With just one year between them, they had always been allies, both fond of Hugo, their elder brother, but both somewhat in awe of him. It was natural enough—Hugo was five years older, a born leader, a touch autocratic, rather conscious of his position as the eldest of all the Perceval children, cousins included. When Hugo went off to London, the two younger ones had become even closer. Hester defended Lowell whenever one of his mad escapades had drawn his parents' wrath down on his head. And when Hester had come back from London in disgrace Lowell had been her chief support.

They were almost at the house before Hester said

finally, 'I'm sorry, Lowell. Seeing Dungarran again reminded me of London. It's wrong to allow myself to be so affected after all these years. I apologise.'

'There's no need for that. But since you mention London… What did you mean when you told him you weren't going there this year? Has Mama given in?'

'Not yet. But I'm still hoping.'

'I doubt she'll change her mind. And if she did, Papa would still have to be convinced. They seem set on giving you another Season, Hes.'

'It's absurd!' said Hester forcefully. 'There's only one reason for taking an unmarried daughter to London for the Season. And since I neither need nor want a husband, the whole exercise will be a waste of money—money the estate can ill afford!'

Lowell put a consoling hand on her arm. 'You might manage to persuade them—but if you don't, things will be different, you'll see. For a start, I'll be there!'

'Oh, that will make all the difference! If I had known the great Lowell Perceval was going to be in London this spring, I would never have argued with Mama. Not for a moment.'

'Hester!'

She smiled at him affectionately. 'I hope you'll have better things to do in London, Lowell, my love, than escort a spinster sister to dances she doesn't wish to attend, or soirées she'd rather die than be seen at! That would be no fun at all, not for you and not for me. No, we can only hope that I am able to change Mama's mind before April comes.'

Meanwhile Robert Dungarran was on the road to London. The weather remained inclement and it was proving a most unpleasant journey. Jolted and tossed as the chaise slipped on the ice and snow, and progress was reduced to walking pace, he had plenty of time to consider. The trip had altogether proved a disappointment. Hunting in the mist, rain and snow of Leicestershire had been dismal, and the society there even less attractive. His trip to Northampton had been a waste of time—he had learned nothing from the Receiving Office. However, it wasn't a matter of great importance, he could put it out of his mind. What was more annoying was the meeting with Hester Perceval... How strange that he hadn't recognised her! When he had first seen her coming round the corner with her cousins she had seemed a different creature altogether. Laughing, animated, capable. It had taken a minute or two to remember what a bore she had been—and the devilishly awkward circumstances of their last meeting... Still, if what she had said about not coming to town for the Season was right, he wouldn't have to see her again... How did Hugo, the most polished of men, and a damned amusing companion, come to have such a dull stick for a sister? Dungarran settled back more comfortably against the squabs and composed himself for sleep...

But sleep eluded him. Memories of Hester Perceval flitted about his mind like ghosts. She was very young, of course, about seventeen. Straight from school. Hugo hadn't wanted her to come to London so early, but the parents had insisted. When was it? 1805—the year of Trafalgar? No, Trafalgar had been the year before. It was 1806...

She had been so quiet at first, a watcher, an observer, with no conversation. They had all wondered what the devil her school had been about. Hugo had said proudly that she was a prize pupil, but the girl hadn't the slightest notion of how to behave in company. She had none of the usual female accomplishments, not even an elementary knowledge of dancing. Out of sympathy for Hugo he had done his best to teach her that, at least. None of the others had volunteered and Hugo had been desperate. Surprisingly enough, it wasn't all that bad. She could be amusing on occasion, and she picked things up quite quickly. You didn't have to tell her anything twice... Except when she refused to listen. He shook his head. She'd been a prize pupil, all right! Before long she had revealed herself as a prize, pigheaded, obstinate little know-all. She was finished after that, of course...

He shifted and made himself more comfortable. They would surely reach Dunstable soon, and then there would be only another day of this nightmare journey. He closed his eyes...

But the memories refused to go away... He hadn't been there when Hugo Perceval's little sister suddenly turned herself into some sort of crusader, bent on reforming the world. Trouble at Portsmouth had kept him out of the capital for a week or two. But when he got back, poor Lady Perceval was distraught, and Hugo was furious.

To begin with everyone was astonished at her impertinence. He grinned as he recalled Lady Scarsdale's outrage,

'Do you know, Robert, that…that *chit* of a girl had the effrontery to ask about the mill in Matlock! I'm sure I haven't the slightest idea what goes on up there, we only visit Derbyshire once or twice a year, and what Arkwright does with his mill is surely his own business. But this…this snip of seventeen—I don't know why I call her a snip, for she's taller than I am—this *pole* of a girl had the audacity to suggest that I *ought* to know how he treats his workers! What on earth is Lady Perceval thinking of, letting such a turniphead loose in society?'

Most of the younger members of the Ton, including himself, just laughed at Hester Perceval—it was impossible to take her seriously. Out of friendship for Hugo, and a sneaking sympathy for the girl, he had done his best to guide her into less stormy waters, but even he had given up in despair. She was bent on her own downfall, stubbornly refusing to listen to hints or even plain speaking. In the end most of the world simply avoided her company. And then had come the Great Scandal, and London had seen her no more.

Shouts and cries made him aware that they had drawn up before the Sugar Loaf in Dunstable. At last!

He got out and stretched himself. He would order a decent meal in a private parlour, have a good night's rest and be in Curzon Street well before dark tomorrow.

The first two of these were accomplished successfully, and Robert Dungarran set off the next day in a better mood. His comfortable home with its self-contained bachelor existence was within reach. But to his annoyance he was unable to rid his mind of the events which had led to Hester Perceval's banishment in 1806…

Society was bored, amused, offended by Miss Perceval, but in the end they had all been deeply shocked by the events at the Sutherlands' ball. He smiled cynically. The gossip hadn't done Canford any good, either, but he deserved what he had got. He should have known better than to complain to the world about a ruined coat after pressing his attentions on an unwilling girl less than a third his age. The man was dead now, but he had been no credit to himself or anyone else. But what, Robert Dungarran wondered, what would society have said if they had known what happened in the Duchess of Sutherland's library *after* the episode with Canford? No one did. No one but Hester Perceval and himself. Thinking back, he had perhaps been harsh with the girl, but encouraging her would have been even more unkind. He shifted uncomfortably, the scene six years before vivid in his mind's eye.

* * *

When Dungarran had arrived at the door of the library Canford had practically knocked him over as he stormed out, swearing vengeance. The noble earl was in a sorry state, his cravat, shirt and velvet coat soaked in wine. Apparently the girl had emptied a glass of the best Bordeaux over him. It looked more like the contents of a decanter. Inside the library he was met with a scene to send any young man of fashion running for cover. Hugo, who was usually calm in all circumstances, had lost his temper spectacularly. Hester, standing in the middle of the room, her bodice torn, and her hair halfway down her back, had been reduced by his words to hysterics. The situation was clearly desperate. When Hugo saw his friend standing in the door he had pleaded, 'Robert, would you take care of this sister of mine? I'll send my mother to her as soon as I can, but she can't leave the room in the state she's in, and I must go after Canford straight away to see what can be done to avoid a scandal.'

With the greatest possible reluctance, Robert, observing the state of both Percevals, had to agree. It was vital that Canford's tirade should be stemmed before too many people heard it, and the girl could not be left alone. Hugo hurried out and he and Hester were left in the room.

'Miss Perceval—'

Hester was now calm enough to speak between her sobs. 'It's all your fault!' she shouted. 'I would never have gone with that…that monster if you had been kinder.'

'Miss Perceval, let me fetch you something to calm you. I'm sorry—'

'I won't listen to your excuses! You all laughed at me, I heard you tonight with your friends! All laughing at me! You're no better than a fashion plate, a pasteboard figure without heart or mind! God might have given you brains, but lack of use has caused them to…to wither away! Don't speak to me! I don't want to hear your excuses!'

Robert Dungarran bowed. 'I was not aware that I had done anything to excuse. But I won't say another word, if that is what you wish.'

'Look at you!' she went on stormily. 'Elegantly empty! You don't care whose heart you break! Making me fall in love with you—'

'Oh no!' This was too much, even for a man of Robert Dungarran's equable temperament. 'That cannot be so. I have never given you the slightest reason to—'

'Of course you did! Why else would you spend so long teaching me to dance, taking me for drives, saying how pretty I looked, when I know very well I am not at all pretty? You are all the same, all of you. Just like Lord Canford—' She was working herself up into hysteria again. Robert had done the only thing possible. He had slapped her, not particularly gently. Eyes wide with shock, she had stared at him.

'You…you monster!' she stuttered. 'To hit a lady…'

'A lady!' he said derisively. 'You! Listen to me, Miss Perceval! You are as close to being a lady as I am to being the Great Cham of China! You are, in fact, an obstinate, conceited, ignorant child. My sympathies, such as they are, are with Hugo. How he came to have such a fool of a sister I cannot imagine. I am sorry the conversation you overheard tonight distressed you, but I would not retract one word from its message. You would do well to persuade your mother to take you away from London to somewhere where you can learn manners and sense in decent obscurity. And now, if you don't mind, I shall guard the door outside until your mother arrives.'

The chaise was passing Hyde Park. He was nearly home, thank God. It was as well. Remembering what he had said to Hester Perceval all those years ago was not a pleasant exercise. The girl had been an appalling nuisance, but he shouldn't have been quite so hard on her. He got out and stretched. Bates, his butler and steward in Curzon Street, was already outside the house, organising the footmen, paying off the chaise and generally being his usual supremely efficient self. It was time to forget Hester Perceval. With any luck he needn't meet her again.

Chapter Two

A few weeks after the trip to Northampton the weather had changed for the better. It was even quite warm. Hester Perceval paid her usual morning calls in Abbot Quincey village, then walked slowly back up the drive to the Hall, which was bathed in early spring sunshine. It was a lovely building of old rose brick decorated with a porch and pilasters of pale grey stone. A wide, graceful flight of steps in the same grey stone led up to its main entrance and two wings of rose brick curved gently to either side. Lawns and tall trees—chestnuts, oaks, ash and holly—surrounded it, though at this time of year most of the trees were bare. But there was a promise of spring in daffodils dancing along the drive, and in the faint haze of green in the hawthorn hedges on the edge of the park.

Hester gazed at it wistfully. Short of a miracle she would soon have to leave the Hall to spend two months or more in the capital. Lady Perceval, normally the most understanding of mothers, had refused to abandon her plan to take her daughter to town in an effort to acquire a husband for her. It was ridiculous! She didn't want a husband—and what was more, she would be extremely surprised if she could find one. But however much she had pleaded, reasoned, even argued, it had been in vain. And now time was scarce. In a few weeks Sir James and Lady Perceval would leave for London, accompanied by their daughter, to take part in the annual carnival which called itself the London Season…Hester quickened her pace up the drive. She must make one last effort to bring her mother to see reason.

But half an hour later Hester was no nearer to success. Her mother was unshaken in her determination, and was growing quite upset by her daughter's obstinate refusal to accept her decision.

'You're a good, clever girl and your father and I love you dearly, Hester. Surely you don't believe that we wish to make you unhappy? Or that we haven't your best interests at heart?' Lady Perceval's voice trembled and her daughter quickly reassured her.

'Of course not, Mama! No one could ask for kinder or more generous parents. It's just… I really don't want another London Season. The last one was enough for me. And surely I'm old enough to know my own mind…'

'Exactly so. You'll be twenty-four in November, Hester! Twenty-four and not a single prospect in view. I did have hopes of Wyndham for you at one time, though he's hardly ever been at Bredington recently. But I hear he has found someone else. And now dear India is married, and Beatrice Roade, too—both very advantageously…'

'But I don't want a husband, Mama! Oh, I wish you would believe me. I could remain a perfectly happy spinster, leading my own life in my own way, if only you would let me.'

'My dear, I've heard all these arguments before, and I assure you yet again, that the only secure future for a woman is in marriage. Or would you prefer to be Hugo's pensioner, once your father and I are no longer here?'

'In no way! Hugo and I would be at odds before the month was out! But in any case that must be a very distant prospect. And I'm sure you could persuade Papa to settle a small amount of money on me instead of taking me to London—' Hester moved over to sit down on the sofa by her mother. She took her hand and looked pleadingly into her parent's unusually determined face. 'If he would give me just a small sum—enough to give me a very modest income—I should be happy to live by myself.'

'Alone?'

'With a maid or…or even a companion if you insisted.'

'Hester, I wouldn't even dream of passing on such a ridiculous notion to your father. And if I did he would laugh it out of court! It's our duty to see you safely married, and a London Season is the best way of doing it.' She looked appraisingly at her daughter. 'You could be quite a good-looking girl, if you would only make the effort. Your dowry, I know, is not large, but there must be someone somewhere who would want to marry you!'

This was too much for Hester's very ready sense of humour. Her mouth twitched as she said demurely, 'Why thank you, Mama! A widower, perhaps, with six children and a wooden leg? He might just be persuaded to take me on.'

'I didn't mean it that way, as you very well know. You are a wicked girl to tease me so. But an older man might be the answer?'

Hester was instantly serious again. 'No, Mama! I do not wish for a husband of any kind—old, young, widowed, single, decrepit, healthy... To put it absolutely plainly, I do not want to marry anyone.'

Lady Perceval looked helplessly at her daughter. 'But *why*, Hester?'

'Because I don't believe there's anyone in the world whom I could respect, and who would be willing to treat me in return as someone capable of rational thought! The polite world is singularly lacking in such men. At least it was six years ago, and I cannot suppose things have changed very much since then. In my experience gentlemen in London only want a pretty face to pay empty compliments to, a graceful partner to dance and flirt with, a...a mirror to tell them in return how witty, how handsome, how elegant they are. And I daresay when they eventually condescend to marry some poor girl, they will treat her like...like a piece of furniture—there to provide an heir and manage the household, while they go their selfish, masculine way, hunting, fishing, shooting and gambling into the night.'

'Hester! Stop, stop! That's quite enough of your nonsense. I won't allow you to say such things when your father is everything that is kind and considerate—you know he is! What other father would allow you to do very much as you please here in Abbot Quincey? Many another would have married you off to some country squire long before now. As it is, he has always respected your wish to live quietly with your books. He is even proud of your work in sorting your grandpapa's papers. He is taking us to London mainly because he honestly believes—as I do—that you would be happier with an establishment and family of your own. We wish to find a husband for you before it is too late.'

'Papa is an exceptional man, Mama, and I admit he has been very patient with me—'

'Well then,' said Lady Perceval, 'why don't you please him—and me—by overcoming your reluctance for another London Season?'

'That wouldn't guarantee a husband for me! Men don't find women like me attractive, Mama. I don't have to remind you of what happened six years ago— you were there.'

Lady Perceval shuddered. 'I was,' she replied with feeling.

'The so-called gentlemen made fun of me! I may have been inept and…and, yes, stupid! But they were so unkind! They made no effort to understand. They couldn't believe that a woman might want to ask questions or debate issues which went beyond the cut of a sleeve or who was whose latest flirt.' She frowned, then shrugged her shoulders and smiled wryly. 'I was foolish to try. The last thing they wanted to do was to be required to think.'

'I've always felt that a lot of the blame was mine, my dear. You were very young. Hugo always advised against taking you straight from Mrs Guarding's Academy into the fashionable world, and he was right. You weren't prepared for it.'

'Mrs Guarding is a wonderful woman. I...'

'I know about Mrs Guarding's advanced views on educating young women. She may be a wonderful teacher, but her ideas do not exactly prepare girls for success in society! You were stuffed full of half-digested notions of saving the world. Praiseworthy, no doubt, but hardly appropriate for the drawing-rooms of the Ton. And then the scandal with Lord Canford ruined everything—'

Hester shuddered. 'Please don't, Mama! If you only knew what that episode did to my self-esteem!'

'I do know! You didn't have a chance after that. I was never so shocked in all my life as when I heard how Canford had behaved at the Sutherlands' ball. Thank heaven Hugo was there to rescue you!'

'He may have saved me from Canford's attentions, but he didn't exactly spare my feelings afterwards—especially when the noble lord aired his grievance to anyone who cared to listen.' A giggle escaped her. 'Mind you, Canford had some cause. If he really believed I had encouraged him, it must have come as a shock when I emptied the glass of wine over him. His coat was ruined. What he must have felt when Hugo came in and caught him chasing me round the room…!'

'I am surprised Canford had so much vitality. He must have been sixty if he was a day!'

'He had a quite remarkable turn of speed. And then Hugo got caught in Canford's walking stick and they both came down. Thank God neither was badly hurt. The scandal would have been even greater if such a prominent member of the aristocracy had been lamed for life by my brother! But Canford limped away quite nimbly in the end. Soaked in wine and cursing.' There was a pause. Then Hester added, 'Looking back now, it was a relief that you were more or less forced to bring me back to Northamptonshire afterwards… I had had enough of London, and Hugo had certainly had enough of me.'

'He was disappointed that his efforts to launch you had failed so disastrously. He suffered too, Hester.'

'My dear Mama, Hugo was far more concerned about his own dignity than he was about my reputation. I'd apparently let him down in front of…in front of…his friends.'

'I'm sure he had forgotten that Dungarran was there when he gave you such a dressing-down. He would never normally have done such a thing in front of anyone else.'

'You believe not?'

'I am sure he wouldn't. It was most unfortunate.

You haven't really been friends with him since, have you, my dear?'

'No. And he comes so seldom to Abbot Quincey now, that there's never an opportunity for us to put things right. Lowell is here quite often, but Hugo never comes.'

Lady Perceval said firmly, 'Hugo is like every other young man of his age—he enjoys life in society. He'll come when he is ready—you'll see. He's thirty in July, and that's when he always said he would settle down.'

'He was so unkind to me! But I miss him, all the same. We were good friends when we were young...' Hester got up, went to the window and gazed at the peaceful scene outside without really seeing it. There was a silence. Then she added bitterly, 'Is it so surprising that I never want to see London again?'

Lady Perceval sighed. 'I am sure things will be different now,' she said persuasively. 'Canford died two years ago. And memories are short.'

'Perhaps. But men still like pretty faces, and dainty, appealing ways in the young women they marry. They don't look for argument or debate. Well, I have never been either pretty or dainty. I'm too tall. And now I'm six years older and my bloom, such as it was, has faded. And, worst of all, though I've lost my passion to change the world, I still enjoy using the brains the Lord gave me in a good argument.' Hester came back to her mother and knelt down beside her. 'Oh Mama, I am convinced that I would never find a husband to please me. I'm perfectly content here in

Abbot Quincey. Please, please will you not speak to Papa?'

Lady Perceval shook her head. 'I would not at this moment even think of making the attempt. Not while there is still time for you to see how wrong you are. Listen to me, Hester,' she went on, gently taking both Hester's hands in hers and speaking very seriously. 'It may surprise you to learn that large numbers of women with considerable intelligence are clever enough to keep themselves and their husbands happy simply by disguising the fact! At seventeen you could be forgiven for not realising this, but not now, Hester. Not now. Look around you! The idea that it is impossible to find happiness in marriage is absurd! I have always been very happy with your dear Papa. And look at Beatrice Roade—a very clever, sensible girl—but since her marriage at Christmas she positively radiates happiness!'

'No one could possibly deny that. But she was lucky. She and Harry Ravensden are exactly right for each other—and Harry doesn't just put up with Mr Roade's eccentricities, he positively delights in them! No, there's no doubt about that marriage, I agree. But that does not change my mind, Mama!'

'And I shall not change mine, Hester. We are going to London for the coming Season.' There was a pause while she looked at her daughter's downcast face. Then her voice softened. 'If nothing has changed by the time we return from London, then we shall see what can be done.'

'Oh, thank you, Mama—'

'But first, you must give yourself another chance,' Lady Perceval said firmly. 'Is it a bargain? Will you promise me to keep an open mind? Will you try to mend fences with Hugo, and forget any grudges from the past? Will you do that?'

'I'll try, Mama,' Hester sighed, 'but it won't be easy.'

'There's my good girl! And now I expect you want to escape to that attic of yours for the rest of the morning, though I'm not at all sure it's good for you to spend so much time alone up there. Wait, Hester! Did you take Mrs Hardwick the eggs when you were in the village? Is she any better?'

'Not yet. But Dr Pettifer will come this afternoon. And the eggs were welcome. They had almost run out.'

'That's good. Off you go, then. You might spend some time reflecting on what I have said. Marriage is a woman's best chance of happiness.'

The way to her attic was long and took her past some of the most beautiful rooms in the house. The family lived in only a small section of the main block, together with a suite of rooms in the west wing occupied by Hester's grandmother. The Dowager Lady Perceval was away at the moment and the rest of the house was silent and unused, the furniture under holland covers, and pictures and ornaments packed away or even sold. Perceval Hall had been built in wealthier times, but Sanford Perceval, Hester's great-grandfather, had been a gambler and a wastrel.

Fortunately he died young, before he had entirely run through the handsome fortune left him by his father. The Percevals no longer owned the vast acres of former days, but they had managed to hold on to the Hall, and their name still counted for something. They were among the county's oldest and most respected landowners, and a Perceval could marry anyone. It was a pity, thought Hester, as she passed large, beautifully proportioned rooms and went up the handsome marble staircase, it was really very unfortunate, that since that London disaster she had been quite unable to imagine sharing her life with any man.

She came at length to her attic. This was her special place, her refuge. She had discovered it years ago, and had made it her own as soon as she found her grandfather's comfortable old chair, and a bureau stuffed full of his books and papers stored there. And when she had returned from London in disgrace, at odds with the world, and out of charity with her much admired elder brother, this was where she had taken refuge. Her parents believed that she was putting her grandfather's papers in order, possibly with a view to publication, and were happy to leave her to it. But, though that was how it had begun, it was far more than that.

For the last five years Hester, wary of exposing herself to yet more mockery for her 'unfeminine' studies, had lived a double life. In public she did what was expected of the daughter of a prominent local family. Though she was regarded as something of a recluse, she rode and walked, worked in the still-room, supported her mother in her charitable work, had frequently visited India Rushford before her marriage to Lord Isham. She was quite often seen in company with her other cousins at the Vicarage. But whenever she could she escaped to her attic. The work on the Perceval papers was nearly finished. But this was not all she did here. And she owed her new occupation to Lowell.

In an effort to rouse Hester from her depression and apathy six years before, Lowell had taken out a subscription for her to Mr Garimond's *Journal of the New Scientific and Philosophical Society.* The fact that the Society was exclusively for gentlemen was disregarded.

Even he could not have foreseen its effect. Hester read it eagerly, and then, greatly daring, sent in a short article on the use of mathematics in ciphers. Lowell had helped to keep her identity secret by delivering it in London himself. To her delight, the article was accepted and for some years now, with Lowell's help, Hester had been sending articles in quite regularly. She called herself 'Euclid', for Mr Garimond insisted that all his contributors used the names of famous mathematicians of the past.

For the past year or more Euclid had been engaged in a duel of wits with 'Zeno', the Journal's senior contributor. Zeno usually wrote scholarly articles on the philosophy of mathematics, but in response to something Hester had written in that first article he had set Euclid a cipher puzzle. He challenged 'him' to solve it before the month was out. This was now a regular feature, Mr Garimond acting as receiving office and umpire. Hester had just finished deciphering the latest, and it would soon go with Lowell to the Society's offices in London.

Lowell was waiting for her in her attic. 'Any luck? Have you managed to persuade Mama? I heard the discussion as I came up.'

'No,' Hester said in a resigned tone. 'I'm to be frizzed and primped and dressed up and paraded in London, somewhat long in the tooth, but apparently still hoping for a husband. Why, pray? So that some man can take me off home and assume he has the right to tell me how to act and what to think. I truly think the world is mad—to condemn, as it does, half of the human race to mindless nonentity. Things will change eventually I suppose—women won't tolerate it for ever. But it won't be in time to save me.'

'Hold on, old thing! Not all men are unreasonable—as you ought to know.' He spoke reproachfully. She went to him and hugged him.

'Oh, don't pay any attention to me, Lowell, I'm just totally out of humour at the idea of going to London again. I'm an ungrateful beast. You've been wonderful. I don't know what I would have done without you. But you wait and see! You're only twenty-two—still reasonably young. Another couple of years in society and you'll be like all the rest.'

'No, I won't,' he said stoutly. 'But people do change in six years, you know. Perhaps some of those fellows might look at you differently now.' Then he added casually, 'I know you have this prejudice about Dungarran, but he seemed very pleasant when we met him in Northampton. He's probably forgotten what happened six years ago.' When his sister remained silent he went on, 'Hester, he can't have been as bad as you think him. Why do you mind him so much? Or was there something more? Something you haven't told me.'

Hester's voice was muffled as she bent over the bureau, searching through her papers. 'Whatever could there be? He was one of Hugo's friends and he did what Hugo asked him. He was kind enough to me until it all went wrong.' She emerged from the bureau, somewhat flushed. 'Did you want something, Lowell?'

'Well, I came to hear Mama's verdict. And I wondered if you had anything for the *Journal*. I'm out for the rest of the day and off to London early tomorrow morning. Have you anything for Garimond? If so, I could deliver it on Friday.'

'Where are you going now?'

'To collect Henrietta from her dancing lesson. I expect I'll spend the rest of the day at the Vicarage.'

Hester suppressed a grin. Lowell had avoided his baby cousin like the plague only months ago, but he was now fascinated by her recent transformation into a very pretty young lady of fashion. She decided not to tease him, but said merely, 'I have something but it isn't quite ready yet. I'll leave it in your room.'

'What is it this time? Another article?'

'No, it's a new cipher they sent me, and I've finally

cracked it. I'm rather pleased with myself, it was quite difficult. You see this line—'

'Don't try to explain, Hes!' Lowell said hastily. 'I'll take your word for it. I wouldn't know where to begin.'

Hester looked at him in some amusement. 'Lowell, however do you convince Garimond that you're the author of these communications? You must meet him occasionally.'

'Never. He's a bit of a mysterious bird himself. But I don't claim to be the author. I just deliver the envelope to an elderly cove at the Society's office in St James's Square.'

'Lucky for us! It saves a few explanations—especially as you are so determined not to be another mathematician!'

'Lord, Hes, I wouldn't know how! But I'd give a lot to know what those clever codgers in St James's Square would say if they knew Euclid was a woman.'

'It would give them all an apoplectic fit! But do take care not to let it out, Lowell—I don't give a pin for their apoplectic fits, but it would mean an end to my fun, too.'

'I won't,' her brother said confidently. 'I like a bit of cloak-and-dagger work. When will the new stuff be ready?'

'It only wants a few corrections and then I'll write it out in my Euclid hand. I'll put it inside your overcoat before I go to bed.'

'Right-eeo.'

Lowell disappeared with a great deal of clattering

down the stairs. Hester shook her head, then smiled fondly. He was a good brother.

She sat down at the bureau, took out her papers and put on her grandfather's spectacles which she had found with his things, and which she now found useful for close work. They never left the attic. But after a few minutes she took them off again and sat back. She was finding it difficult to concentrate. It was Lowell's fault for mentioning Dungarran's name. That and the knowledge that she could not avoid seeing the man again in London... Lowell was right. She hadn't told him everything. There was one scene that no one knew of. No one but herself and Dungarran. It wasn't surprising that she had wished never to face him again. He had appeared to be so kind, so interested in her—until she had found him out. It had very nearly broken her heart to find that her idol had feet of such poor clay... And even then she had refused to accept it. Hester's eyes strayed to the tiny window, but what she saw was not the green fields and trees of Northamptonshire but the drawing-rooms and streets of London in 1806...

Hester Perceval's preparation for her début at seventeen was unusual. Her talents in the drawing-room were no more than adequate, but Mrs Guarding, a woman with advanced views on the education of women, had taken great pride in Hester's gift for languages and her agile mind. She had encouraged Hester to believe that an intelligent, informed woman could create interest in badly needed reforms, bring the rich, particularly those in London and the south, to appreciate the difficulties of the poor in the north.

An older and wiser Hester now knew better. Mrs Guarding was usually the most astute of women, but in Hester's case her enthusiasm had overcome her judgement. Social change has been brought about by intelligent women. But such women have been mature, sophisticated matrons with an established position, women of tact and experience who know their world, not naïve seventeen-year-olds with a strong sense of mission and no idea how to handle it.

All had gone well for the first few weeks after Hester's arrival in London in the spring of 1806. Her adored brother Hugo was ready to look after her and introduce her to his circle of friends, all of them prominent in the Ton. Feminine enough to enjoy the pretty dresses her mother had provided for her, she accepted with pleased surprise the compliments the gentlemen paid her on her appearance. Fascinated by life in the metropolis, at first she spoke little and observed much. She soon came to the conclusion that Mrs Guarding was right. Though society had been kind to her, it was all too frivolous, too uncaring. As soon as she had found her feet, she would start her campaign…

Meanwhile it was very pleasant to be looked after by Hugo's friends. It took a little time for her to become accustomed to their languid drawls, their refusal to take anything seriously, but it was flattering to a girl not yet eighteen to be attended by some of the most eligible young men in society. Even Dungarran, famous for his reluctance to put himself out for any-one—'Too fatiguin'!' was his favourite phrase—spent time teaching her the dance steps she had ignored at Mrs Guarding's. Elegant, handsome, with dark hair and cool grey eyes, he spoke less than the others, seldom paying her the pretty compliments she came to expect, but this did him no harm in Hester's opinion. There was an occasional glimmer of amusement in his eyes which intrigued her, but it was usually quickly replaced by his normal, indifferent courtesy. Though he evaded all her attempts at serious conversation, Hester was certain that behind the idle man of fashion there was an intelligence, an intellect she could respect. Inevitably, sadly, she was soon on the way to falling in love with him. She found herself listening for his lazy drawl, searching the crowds for a sight of his tall figure, always so immaculately dressed, rivalling Hugo in his calm self-possession. But though he was instantly welcome wherever he went, invited to every function, he was not always to be found. He seemed to come and go very much as he pleased. And as time went on he became even more elusive. Without him, life in London soon became very boring to Hester.

After a month, finding most conversations, even the compliments, tediously repetitive, she began her campaign. She would interrupt a frivolous discussion on the newest fashion for a collar, or Beau Brummell's latest *bon mot*, in order to comment on the condition of the workers in the north, or the passage of a bill for reform through Parliament. This was met with blank stares. When invited out for a drive she took to lecturing her companion on the greater role women could, and would, play in public life, or expressing a desire to be taken to the poorer districts of London in order to observe living conditions there. Needless to say, no one ever took her, but even the request caused the lifting of eyebrows...

Her mother saw what was happening but found herself powerless to stop it. Her remonstrances, her pleas to Hester to stop trying to reform society until she was better informed of its manners and customs, fell on deaf ears. Hugo warned her, his closer friends did their best to deflect her, but Hester remained obstinately idealistic, stubbornly sure that intelligent discussion could solve the problems of the world... The result was inevitable. Society began to ignore, then neglect her. The flow of compliments, the invitations to drive or ride, dried up quite suddenly as Miss Perceval was pronounced guilty of the worst sin of all. She was a bore. And not even a pretty one.

Chapter Three

At first Hester was puzzled rather than distressed. The young men around her had listened so charmingly. They had paid her such pretty compliments, taken such pleasure in her company. What was wrong? Why didn't they want to listen to her?

The awakening was painful. Alone, as she so often was, on a balcony overlooking one of the rooms in the Duchess of Sutherland's mansion, half hidden by long curtains, she heard a burst of laughter from below and then voices.

'I don't believe it! You must be making it up, Brummell! Are you trying to tell us that Hester Perceval actually took Addington to task on the question of Catholic emancipation? Addington!'

'My dear chap, every word of it is true, I swear.' Hester looked cautiously over the balcony. Seven or eight young gentlemen were gathered underneath. She drew quickly back.

'Oh God!' There was despair in Hugo's voice. 'What has she done now? What did he say?'

George Brummell was a born mimic. Addington's self-important tones were captured perfectly. 'My dear Miss Perceval, how you can think I would discuss policies of His Majesty's Government with an impertinent chit of a girl I cannot imagine. And why the devil you should see fit to mention such a subject in Lady O'Connell's drawing-room has me even more at a loss.'

Shouts of laughter, and applause. Then Hester strained forward as she heard Robert Dungarran's drawl.

'Poor girl! I know that blistering tone of Addington's.'

'Come, come, Robert! Little Miss Cure-all deserved the set-down. She's an impudent ninny. What have politics to do with a woman? Their little brains simply aren't up to it!'

'Do tell me, George—are yours?'

More laughter, and the good-natured reply. 'I've never tried t' fathom them—even if my health permitted me to try. Fatiguin' things, politics. All the same, Hugo, isn't it time you did something about the girl?'

'Quite right, Brummell!' The interruption came from Tom Beckenwaite. 'Dammit, when I'm with a woman I don't want to think—that's not what they're for!' He gave a low laugh, which was followed by a chorus of ribald remarks. Hester was shocked. She had always regarded Lord Beckenwaite as a true gentleman. A fool, but a gentlemanly fool. He spoke again.

'The fact is, Hugo, old dear, you are wasting your time. Your little sister is incurable. And unmarriage-able. Demme, there's a limit to what a fellow can stand! I'm as ready as the next man to do a friend a favour, but your sister is demned hard work, and that's not something I look for. She never stops talkin'! Ridin', drivin', dancin'—it's all the same! Talk, talk, talk!'

'Hugo—' Hester leaned forward again. This was Dungarran speaking. She smiled in anticipation. He would defend her against these asses. He seldom spoke but when he did it was always to the point. They would listen to him. His drawl was more pro-nounced than ever. 'Hugo, I'm sorry to say it, but it's time you did something!'

'Not you too, Robert!' Hugo said resignedly.

'Have a word with Lady Perceval, old chap. Your wretched sister's behaviour is doing neither herself, nor anyone else, much good. She is too young, and much too foolish for life here. Get your mother to take her back to Nottingham, or Northampton or wherever it is you all come from. Perhaps the country air will blow away some of her silly notions. Bring her back when she's learned how to behave. But, please, not before.'

Hugo said stiffly, 'She never used to be like this, and I'm sorry for it. I don't know what my mother was thinking of, bringing her to London with her head full of such nonsense.'

'It's not nonsense, exactly. Just absurd coming from your sister.' Dungarran again. 'It would be better suited to a graybeard with a corporation than a child out of the schoolroom. A girl into the bargain.'

'I don't know what to say to you all. She's my sister and I love her, I suppose. But believe me, when I asked you all to give her a good start to the Season I never imagined it would be such hard work. You've been Trojans.'

'Well, from now on, dear boy, your sister can lecture someone else. This Trojan is retiring to his tent. Wounded in the course of duty, you might say. Shall we look for the card-room?' A chorus of agreement faded as they went away, leaving Hester sitting in her chair staring into space. How could they talk of her like that! How dare they! Shallow, stupid... It was as if a veil had been ripped from her eyes. She could now see that their smiles had been sly, their compliments mere flattery, their attentions empty... She drew in a shuddering breath. They were all fools! Every one of them! Fashionable fools with no more brain than a pea! Heartless, brainless fools!...

'You're looking serious, my dear. Are you alone?'

She looked up. An elderly gentleman was gazing at her in concern. His face was vaguely familiar.

'Sir...' she stammered. 'You must excuse me. I...I am a little...a little...' Her voice faded.

'My dear girl, you are clearly upset. How fortunate that I happened on your hiding place. Come. You shall have something to restore you, and then I shall take you back to your Mama. Or...' He eyed her speculatively. 'Perhaps you would tell me more of the very interesting reforms in the north you've been studying?'

Hester looked at him in surprise. 'I've talked to you before? I'm afraid…'

'No, but I was there when you were talking about them to Lady Castle. I found them quite absorbing. May I know more?'

This was balm to Hester's wounded pride. Here was a man of mature years, obviously distinguished, who, far from laughing at her, respected her views enough to want to hear more! What a contrast to those…fribbles of Hugo's, especially Dungarran! Here was someone who really appreciated her.

They talked for a moment or two, and never since she came to London had Hester had such an attentive listener. After a moment he winced as a burst of music came from below, and said, 'I hardly dare suggest it, but we would be more private in the library. Of course, if you don't care for the idea we could continue to sit here…'

The temptation to sit there on the balcony, to be seen by people who did not appreciate her as they ought, was very strong. But he went on, 'The Duchess has a splendid selection of books on the subject…?'

Books! She hadn't seen a book in weeks! Hester smiled and nodded with enthusiasm. She was too shy to ask him his name, but he clearly knew her family. There could be nothing wrong in accepting the invitation from such a very distinguished-looking old man. The cane he used to support him was of ebony with a silver-chased top. His coat was of blue velvet and the ribbon and diamonds of some sort of order was pinned to its front. His white hair was tied back in the old-fashioned way with a velvet ribbon. He was altogether the epitome of august respectability. Filled with pride at having attracted the attention of such a man, she accepted the arm he offered and let him guide her through the doors and on into the library. He led her to a sofa by the window. On a table next to it was a decanter filled with wine, and some glasses.

'Sit down, Miss Perceval. Will you have some wine?'

'I'm not sure… Why did you shut the door?'

'Do you not find the noise outside disturbing? You are young, of course. Your hearing is more acute than mine. Would you like me to open it again?'

'Oh no!'

'Good! Let me pour you some wine.' He smiled at her reassuringly in a grandfatherly way.

'Th…thank you.' Hester smiled nervously at him. He handed her a large glass of wine at which she gazed apprehensively, then came round and sat down beside her.

'Now, tell me why you think the north needs special attention. Are things there so very different from the south?'

'Oh, they are!' Relieved, Hester launched into a description of conditions in the manufacturing towns. She was flattered by the attention the gentleman was paying to her words, and failed to notice at first how very close to her he was sitting, his arm along the back of the sofa. It seemed very warm in the room, and she was relieved when he got up and walked over to one of the bookcases. But her relief was short-lived. When he returned with a heavy volume, he sat even more closely, his thigh pressing against hers.

'We shall look at this together,' he said with a smile, and opened the page at a spectacularly un-dressed lady...

Even today, six years later, she could still feel the shock. She had sat paralysed for a moment, and Canford had taken the opportunity to turn her head to his... His lips came down on hers with brutal force, his tongue forcing its way into her mouth. One hand clutched the front of her bodice... With a scream of outrage and horror she had leapt away, snatched up her glass of wine, which was still very full, and emptied it over him. She made for the door.

Canford was beside himself with rage. 'My coat! Look at my coat, you damned little vixen!' he snarled, picking up his stick and lifting it threateningly as he chased after her. She managed to unlock the door before he reached her, but then he grabbed her hair and wrenched it painfully as he pulled her back.

She screamed again, whereupon the door burst open, knocking her aside, and Hugo rushed in. What happened next was a blur, but it ended with Canford and her brother crashing to the floor together. It was a dangerous moment, luckily interrupted by the arrival of Robert Dungarran.

'Canford! Hugo!'

Canford, recalled to sanity by Dungarran's inter-vention, got up, glared at Hugo, and stormed out, swearing vengeance on all concerned.

Hugo then turned to her. After making sure she was unharmed, he lost his temper with her—comprehen-sively. The general drift was that he had finished with her. She had ruined not only herself, but the rest of the family in the eyes of the Ton. After a few other, similarly amiable sentiments, he had gone out after Canford to see, he snapped, whether he could limit the damage she had caused. She had been left, ashamed and humiliated, alone with Dungarran.

Hester preferred not to think of what had fol-lowed—the recriminations, the accusations, her stupid declaration of love, and his contemptuous rejection of her. If she was to meet Dungarran in April with any degree of equanimity she must put that scene out of her mind. Forget it completely.

Hester picked up the pen, put on her glasses and returned to work. This was what was important, what would be important in the future. She finished her copying and sealed the papers up. Recently Garimond had insisted that every precaution should be taken to keep her work from prying eyes. She always com-plied, though she couldn't see a reason for it. Men were basically very childish with their secrets and their ciphers. The messages Zeno had sent her re-cently had all been to do with Romans marching into Gaul, and transport over the Alps. Did he regard him-self as a latter-day Caesar? Some of it didn't even make sense. But he was clever! His ciphers had always been devilishly ingenious, even the simpler ones he used for his covering letters... These were never published, of course.

Hester gave a little laugh. Who would think that Hester Perceval, spinster and recluse, would dare to conduct a secret correspondence with an unknown gentleman? Even parents as indulgent as hers would be shocked beyond measure at it. But Zeno could hardly be regarded as a danger, even by the strictest guardians, for, in the nature of things, she and Zeno would, regrettably, never meet! Though she felt a surprising sense of kinship with him, an astonishing similarity of humour and ideas, she could never reveal her true identity. The shock would probably kill the elderly gentleman, who sat in his club in St James, painstakingly writing his articles, and inventing the most tortuous, the most diabolically difficult ciphers—all for a woman to solve!

Hester's eyes wandered over her attic and stopped at a dusty cupboard in the corner. Should she open it? Inside was the manuscript of *The Wicked Marquis*, a ridiculous novel she had written in fury after her return in the summer of 1806. Her pen might well have been dipped in vitriol, so corrosive had been the caricatures of her unsuspecting victims. No, it was better left locked away where no one else could read it. She would otherwise face ruinous actions for libel! One day she would destroy it. But writing *The Wicked Marquis* had undoubtedly helped her recovery. Through its absurdities she had learned to laugh not only at society, but also at herself at seventeen—naïve, arrogant, so sure that she could change the world... She smiled as she thought of the absurd plot based on tales told by the servants of the local villain, the Marquis of Sywell—the orgies in the chapel, the deflowering of local maidens, the mysterious disappearance of the Marchioness... She had surrounded him with vain, empty-headed young men with ridiculous names, caricatures of the men she had met in London—even Hugo had not escaped. The Marquis of Rapeall, Sir Hugely Perfect, Viscount Windyhead—he had hardly deserved her malice, he had been scarcely older than herself—Lord Baconwit, the dandy Beau Broombrain and—Lord Dunthinkin.

Which brought her back to Dungarran. Hester straightened her shoulders and lifted her chin. At seventeen she had gone to London expecting the world to fall at her feet. At twenty-four she expected very little—merely to get through the Season with as little trouble as possible. Then she would return and continue her relationship with the only man she respected—Zeno. He was the man for her.

Lady Perceval was delighted when her daughter agreed to accompany them to London without further protest. She launched into a frenzy of discussions with the local dressmakers—already working at full capacity on Robina Perceval's wardrobe. The house was swamped in samples and pattern books. It soon became clear that they would unfortunately not get to town in time for Sophia Cleeve's come-out ball. This was held in March, and it was the middle of April before Sir James brought his wife and daughter to the house Hugo had found for them off Berkeley Square.

'Very pleasant!' pronounced Lady Perceval, looking round her as the family entered the spacious salon on the first floor. 'How clever of you, Hugo dear, to find such a pleasant house in such a convenient situation. Hester, do you not agree?'

Mindful of her promise, Hester smiled at her brother and offered her cheek. 'I would expect nothing less,' she said, as he kissed it. 'I'm glad to see you, brother. You're looking well—and very elegant.'

'I was delighted to hear you had agreed to come, Hester. I think we can do better this time, don't you?'

Hester sighed. 'I'll try, Hugo. I'll try. I can at least promise not to make a nuisance of myself.'

'We'll do better than that,' he promised, smiling down at her with a glint in his eye. Her heart warmed to him. When Hugo forgot he was a nonpareil with a position to uphold, there was no one kinder or more affectionate. The older brother she had loved was still there, underneath the man of fashion.

Lowell came bounding up the stairs, falling over some valises on the way, and the mood of family unity was disturbed.

'I'm sorry, Mama, Papa,' he gasped. 'I meant to be here when you arrived.'

'Ma'am,' said Hugo impatiently, turning to his mother. 'Ma'am, I wish you would persuade your younger son to be less…less noisy! It's like having a Great Dane in the drawing-room!'

Sir James laughed. 'Let him be, Hugo! He'll learn. How are you, my boy?'

'Well, sir, very well. I find London greatly to my taste—especially since I moved out of Sir Hugely Perfect's rooms. Sharing with Gaines is much more fun.'

Hester's start of surprise fortunately went unnoticed as Sir James said disapprovingly, 'What was that you said? Sir Hugely Perfect? That is not amusing, Lowell. It doesn't do to call your brother names.'

'Oh, I'm not alone, sir! That's how he is known here in London.'

'Sir Hugely Perfect?' Lady Perceval went over to her son. 'Hugo! How unkind! Are you really called so?'

The colour had risen in Hugo's cheeks, but he shrugged his shoulders and laughed. 'Not by everyone, only Lowell and his cronies. The rest of my acquaintance are not so childish.'

Hester cleared her throat. 'Where…where did such a name come from, Lowell? Mama is right. It isn't kind.'

'It's from a book,' Hugo answered for Lowell, who had hesitated. 'A piece of rubbish which came on the scene a month or two ago. But no one of any sense could possibly take it seriously.'

'A book?'

Lowell held his sister's eyes. 'A book called *The Wicked Marquis*. And Hugo is mistaken. It's not just my set. The whole of the beau-monde is talking about it.'

Lady Perceval was looking bewildered. '*Hugo?* A wicked marquis? What *are* you talking about, Lowell?'

'Hugo isn't the wicked marquis, Mama. He's just a character in the book. One of a great number.'

Hester said faintly, 'Mamà, I should quite like to see my room. I feel sadly dishevelled, and…and I have a touch of the headache.'

'My poor child! I thought you seemed rather pale— we rose so early this morning, Hugo. I dare swear you were not even awake when we left Perceval Hall. Come, my dear!' At the door she paused. 'I hope to see you later, Hugo. Are you dining here?'

'Certainly! I couldn't neglect you all on your first evening in town. I must bring you up to date! Sophia Cleeve's ball was a huge success, by the way. No expense spared, naturally. And in her quiet way little Robina is doing very well.'

'Excellent! Excellent!' Sir James beamed with pleasure.

His wife was equally pleased. She left Hester and came back into the room to join Hugo and her husband. 'What a relief for her mother!' she exclaimed. 'Elizabeth was so worried at the expense of it all, but if Robina can make a reasonable match, the prospect for her sisters is vastly improved. She is, of course, a very pretty girl. Do you know who…?'

Hester seized her opportunity. She pulled Lowell out into the hall and pushed him into a side room, shutting the door firmly behind them. Then she turned.

'What have you done, Lowell?' she hissed.

'I don't know what you m—'

Hester gave her brother a most unladylike shake.

'Yes you do, you little toad! How did you find it? And what did you do with it?'

'Oh, you mean *The Wicked Marquis*? I sold it.'

'You *what*?'

'I sold it. I showed it to a friend of mine in Cambridge and he was as keen as mustard about it. He knew where to go to get it printed, and…'

'You…you sold it? For publication? You're trying to hoax me, Lowell—no respectable publisher would handle a thing like that!'

'Well, no. That's where old Marbury was so useful. He knew a fellow who dealt with the other kind.'

'Lowell!' Hester was horrified, but Lowell was too full of enthusiasm to notice.

He went on, 'It needed spicing up a bit for that kind of trade, of course, so I did that. I brought it up to date as well. I didn't do at all a bad job, either. The chap I sold it to was quite impressed.'

'You…you *traitor*, Lowell! How could you! How *dare* you!'

He looked injured. 'I thought you'd be pleased. It wasn't doing any good in that dusty old cupboard, and now it's a huge success. Don't listen to what Hugo says. It's not just my set—*everyone* is talking about it.'

'Oh God!' she said in despair, pacing up and down in a fever of anxiety. 'Oh, Lowell! How could you? We're ruined!'

'Nonsense! For one thing, no one knows who the author is—'

'But they're bound to find out! It wouldn't be difficult to work out who wrote it—all the people in it were the ones *I* knew. I'm surprised Hugo hasn't worked it out already.'

'That's where my bits came in,' said her brother proudly. 'I think you'll find that I've obscured the tracks enough.'

'I must see it—immediately. Tonight!'

'I don't think so, Hes. Gaines and I are off to Astley's tonight. Tomorrow.'

'You'll bring it tonight, you snake—'

'Hester!' Lady Perceval came into the room. 'I thought you had gone upstairs. Whatever are you doing here? And Lowell!'

'I... I...er... I have some messages for Lowell. From the Vicarage.'

'Henrietta, perhaps?' asked her mother with a significant smile. 'I won't ask what they are—you obviously want to deliver them in private. Lowell, shall we see you tonight?'

Her two children answered at the same time. 'Yes!' said Hester. 'No, unfortunately not,' said Lowell with an apologetic smile. Sir James, hearing this, was annoyed.

'What's this, sir? Your mother and I would have liked you to be here!'

'Sorry, Papa! It's Gaines. He's leaving town tomorrow. He has to go down to Devon for a few weeks. Tonight's the only night we can go and we've been promising ourselves this treat for ages. I'll be here tomorrow morning—about noon.'

With this his parents had to be content, though they were not best pleased. As they turned to go Hester, who had been thinking furiously, said, 'Mama, Lowell has suggested we go for a short walk. He thought that might relieve my headache better than lying in a stuffy room. I should dearly like to see where he lives. I know it isn't far. Just round the corner…almost.' She gave Lowell a sweet smile. Only he could sense the determination behind it.

'Well…'

'I'm sure he'll look after me, Mama. Won't you, Lowell?'

'Of course! If you're sure you want to…'

'I want to. May I, Mama?'

A few moments later Hester was accompanying Lowell to Half Moon Street. After a silence she said, 'You haven't told me yet how you discovered it.'

Lowell had had time to reflect on Hester's reaction. He had genuinely thought that it was a wonderful jest to have her book published, but now he was no longer so sure. It was a long time since he had seen Hester in such a rage.

'I… I was waiting for you in the attic. This was some time ago, Hes. You were a long time coming. So…so I explored. The key was on top of the cupboard, and…and…'

'You opened it. And stole the manuscript.'

'Don't say that! I read it on the spot. It isn't very long, as you know. If you had come in then I daresay

I shouldn't have done anything with it. But you were held up in the village or something, so I had plenty of time to finish it. I couldn't stop laughing. It was brilliant!'

'Laughing!' Hester exclaimed bitterly.

'Well, I daresay you didn't feel like laughing when you wrote it. But your caricatures were hilarious to an outsider. And one or two of them hit the nail right on the head. That's why it's such a wild success. All London is laughing. I don't know why you're taking it so badly, Hester!'

'Lowell! If it ever comes out that I wrote the thing then I am dished—completely. For ever! London won't laugh then. They'll hunt me out of town.'

'They won't find out. I told you, I altered it to disguise your part. And…and…'

'Continue, little brother,' said Hester ominously when Lowell hesitated.

'Well, I put things in it that a respectable girl couldn't possibly know about. You'd mentioned some of Sywell's escapades—you remember that party no one would talk about, until I got old Silas to tell? And the business with Abel Bardon's daughters? You didn't know the details—no one would tell you, of course, so you'd used your imagination. Well, I just added a few of the real facts. No one could possibly believe you knew anything about those.'

Hester stopped and put her hands over her face. 'Lowell, this is the worst thing you have ever done to me. I can't bear it!' she said.

Lowell took her arm, aware of the curious glances

directed at them both. He said in a low voice, 'The situation isn't nearly as bad as you think, Hester. Look! We're nearly at my place—come in and I'll give you something—a glass of wine, perhaps? Gaines has some first-class burgundy.'

Hester allowed herself to be shepherded into the small house in Half Moon Street where Lowell had his rooms. 'I'd like to drown you in it. But I'll have some water, or possibly some tea. Not wine.'

'I say, Hester! That's not fair! I did it for a lark!'

'That's what you always say, Lowell! But this is no lark!' Her brother's air of injured innocence, rather like that of a hurt puppy, was having its usual effect. Hester was never able to stay angry with Lowell for long. But when she looked at the book which Lowell put into her hands a few minutes later she exploded again.

'This is disgusting!'

'Well, yes. They did spread themselves on the cover. The Marquis is being really astonishingly wicked.' As Lowell looked at it he started to grin appreciatively. 'I don't know how the devil he managed that position, though.'

'Lowell!! You shouldn't be showing me this…this filth! You shouldn't even be mentioning such things to me! Oh Lord! I can't believe this is happening to me. Not another disaster, not again!' Hester was distraught. She walked up and down the room in agitation.

'Oh come, Hester! I may have spiced the novel up a little—'

'A little! If this is anything to go by...'

'A lot, then. But you can't go all prunes and prisms on me. After all, you thought it all up. I only embellished it.'

'Oh no!'

'And the cover is the worst thing about it. It's really not so lurid inside. Read it and see for yourself. I promise you, it will make you laugh.'

'I shall do nothing of the sort!' She stopped short. Then she wailed, 'I shall have to read the confounded thing! Tonight, if possible. I must see what you've done to it. Lowell, I shall never forgive you for this, never! Here, take the book and wrap it up—properly, mind! I don't want it to come undone before I can hide it in my room.'

Lowell was now so anxious to please that he wrapped the offending book into a small parcel and handed it over. 'I'll escort you back,' he said contritely.

'No! I don't want your company! I'm used to walking alone, and it's only a step.'

'But I must—'

'Lowell,' said Hester with awful calm. 'Don't argue with me. I shall scream if I have to say another word to you! I need to walk back to Bruton Street *alone*! I just might be able to speak to you tomorrow, but don't count on it.' She turned and left him standing on the door step. He waited irresolutely, then shrugged his shoulders and went in.

Hester walked swiftly back up towards Berkeley Square. She was seething with an explosive mixture

of anger and apprehension. How dare Lowell do such
an outrageous thing! What would become of her—
and her family—if London ever found her out? The
parcel in her hand seemed to burn through to her fingers; she wanted to drop it, but dared not let it go.
She reached the top of Half Moon Street and turned
in the direction of Berkeley Square, head down, still
clutching her parcel—and collided with a tall gentleman who was coming towards her. She dropped her
parcel and with a gasp of dismay bent down to pick
it up. A hand came out to prevent her.

'You must allow me,' said a deep, drawling voice.

Hester groaned inwardly. Fate was always against
her on such occasions. It was inevitable that out of
all the gentlemen in society she should meet *this* one,
just when she least wanted to. She summoned up her
courage. 'Lord Dungarran!' she exclaimed.
'How…how…pleasant to meet you again!'

Chapter Four

Surprise, a fleeting expression of resignation, and then a faint hint of reproof—Hester saw all of these cross Dungarran's face before he resumed his normal calm.

'Miss Perceval. What an unexpected pleasure!'

The words were conventional, and were not supported by any warmth in his voice. Hester's eyes dropped. He must not be allowed to see the panic into which Lowell's revelations had thrown her. Not this man.

'Thank you for coming once again to my rescue, sir,' she said stiffly and held out her hand for the parcel.

He smiled briefly, but did not hand it over. 'At least it isn't wet.' His eyes surveyed the street. 'But…are you once again in need of an escort, Miss Perceval?'

'Not in the slightest. I am making for Berkeley Square. It isn't far.'

'All the same,' he said decidedly, 'I will accompany you.' He offered her his arm.

'It really isn't necessary, Lord Dungarran. If you will give me my parcel I am perfectly able to walk the few yards to the square.'

He frowned. 'Miss Perceval, I have no wish to force my company on you, believe me. But you may be assured that if your parents or Hugo knew that you were walking the streets of London without a maid or footman they would be as…surprised as I am. It is bad enough in Northampton. In London it is un-heard of. Come!' He presented his arm again.

The colour rose in Hester's cheeks. There was so much she wanted to say, none of it polite. So she remained silent, her eyes fixed anxiously on the parcel which he still carried in his other hand. She was faintly surprised not to see signs of scorching on its wrappings. As they walked along Curzon Street he held it out and said, 'What is it this time, Miss Perceval? Not muslin or satin—it is too hard for that. Or should I not ask? It feels like a book.'

Hester swallowed and tried to smile. 'It…it is a book. Lowell has lent me a book of…of…poetry. B—ballads.'

'You like poetry?'

'I… I… No, I don't.'

She heard him give a slight sigh. Then he began again, patiently making conversation with someone, she thought resentfully, he would much rather not have to talk to at all. If he only knew the strain she was under to say even a word that was sensible!

'Have you been in London long, Miss Perceval?'

'No. We have just arrived.'

'Ah!'

They entered Berkeley Square in silence. He paused. 'You are fortunate in finding a suitable house in the square. They are much in demand. Which is it?'

She disengaged herself. 'We…we are staying in Bruton Street, in fact. A few yards farther on. But you have done enough, Lord Dungarran. Thank you. May I have my book?' He gave her a look and offered her his arm again.

Still in silence they crossed the square. To Hester's relief the entrance to the house was in sight. She began to thank him again, holding out her hand for the book. 'No, Miss Perceval. I shall see you to your door,' he said grimly, ignoring her attempts at farewell.

At the door he bowed and at last handed her the parcel. 'Goodbye, Miss Perceval. No doubt we shall see each other again.'

'I look forward to it already,' said Hester.

He narrowed his eyes at her tone, then added coldly, 'Meanwhile, I would remind you that it is unwise to go out alone in London—as I am sure Hugo would tell you if he were here.'

It was too much! Hester lifted her chin and said in a high voice, 'Lord Dungarran, I am grateful for your solicitude for someone who is, after all, the merest acquaintance. I assure you that I shall do my utmost in the future not to put you to any more trouble, however unnecessary. Goodbye.' She curtseyed and went in.

* * *

As Robert Dungarran retraced his steps towards Curzon Street a slight frown marred his handsome features. The years had apparently not improved Hester Perceval. She was still uncomfortable in society, inept in conversation, and obstinate in her opinions. It was to be hoped that Hugo would not call on him again for support in looking after his sister. He would have to refuse. He walked on a little, then paused in thought. For someone who had so little command of language her last remark had been remarkably polished. In two sentences she had thanked him, accused him of unwarranted interference, and made it clear that she would avoid him in the future! And now he thought of it, her 'I look forward to it already' had been delivered with a nice touch of irony. Was there more to Hester Perceval than at first appeared…? Impossible! He strode on.

Meanwhile Hester, still clutching her parcel, had scurried up two flights of stairs. She had managed to avoid the servants, who would have taken her pelisse and hat, and had arrived, breathless, in her bedchamber. It was a charming little room decorated in blue and pale yellow, with a window from which she could just see a corner of the gardens in the centre of Berkeley Square. It was growing dark outside. But Hester had no eyes for any of this. In haste she hid the book, still in its wrappings, among the papers she had brought with her. The servants would not interfere with those. Then she called for her maid and quickly changed her dress for dinner. She eventually arrived in the drawing-room just as her mother was remarking on her absence.

'Ah, there you are, Hester! I was almost coming to see what had happened to you. Did you enjoy your walk with Lowell?'

'Yes, Mama. His rooms are very agreeable.'

'Did you meet the famous Mr Gaines?'

'No—I gather he is seldom in. In any case, Mama, I shouldn't raise your hopes if I were you. I'm afraid Mr Gaines is useless as a prospective husband. After tonight he will be in Devon for most of the Season, and I doubt I shall see him again.'

'Good gracious, Hester, nothing was further from my mind. Did…did Lowell see you safely back?'

'Er…no, Mama. I left him at his rooms.'

'You can't have walked alone. And you didn't take one of the footmen. Who was that with you at the door?'

Her mother would be most upset to learn that she had set out from Half Moon Street without an escort. Hester said, 'Lord Dungarran kindly offered to accompany me.'

'Indeed? A very good friend of Hugo's. And a most eligible *parti*.' She smiled benevolently at her daughter.

'Not as far as I am concerned, Mama.'

Lady Perceval gave a sigh of exasperation. 'Hester, I am quite sure you need have no apprehension about Hugo's friends. They have surely all forgotten the events of six years ago. You must forget them, too.

Simply behave as if this were your first visit to London, and you will do very well.' She paused, then went on, 'Dungarran appeared to be most attentive…'

There was a pause during which Hester tried to think of something to say. Her mother went on, 'It is a great pity that you went out this afternoon straight from your journey. If I had not been so interested in what Hugo was telling us I would have made you change your dress. Your pelisse was sadly crushed. I cannot imagine what Dungarran thought of it.'

'Mama, Dungarran is interested neither in my dress, nor in my person. Please do not imagine differently.'

Lady Perceval ignored her. She went on, 'That dress looks very well, my dear. But I must have a word with your abigail. Your hair is not at all well arranged.'

Since she had allowed her maid a mere three minutes for the task Hester was not surprised. She looked down. She had no idea what she was wearing. The dress consisted of a straight slip with an overskirt and sleeves of dull green. There had been much discussion during its making about her lack of curves, which had resulted in a lavish use of lace round the top of the bodice. She sighed. It was difficult to be enthusiastic about clothes when one was tall and skinny. Her cousin Robina could look appealing in a kitchenmaid's sack apron—not that Aunt Elizabeth, whose notions of propriety were very strict, would ever allow her daughter to be seen in one.

'Hester?'

'Oh, I'm sorry, Mama! I was wool-gathering. You were saying?'

'When Hugo arrives we shall decide what events we shall attend. There are several cards already here, and others are sure to come. In addition, your father and I plan to hold a couple of soirées. Hugo will help us to draw up a guest list… We must make sure Dungarran's name is included.'

Hester was about to protest, then she decided to hold her peace. The noble lord was almost sure to find himself 'unable to attend'! Her thoughts wandered again. How boring it all was! And all for nothing. Her encounter this afternoon had brought home to her once again how unfitted she was for life in society. How uninterested she was in life in society! Worse still, she was racked with anxiety about the book. As soon as she could she would escape and read the thing this evening. It was not something she looked forward to.

Nothing occurred during the next week to change Hester's opinion of society. She dutifully attended dinners, parties, soirées, balls, where she exchanged platitudes, pretended an interest she didn't feel in the latest styles or the latest engagements—and danced. She even danced once or twice with Lord Dungarran. Much as she still disliked him, she had to admit he was an agreeable partner. Their steps fitted very well. She only wished that she could demonstrate how much she had changed from the 'obstinate, conceited, ignorant child' he had called her all those years ago.

But she found she could not do it. His patent indifference, and her own lingering dislike and resentment, were in the way. And, from what she had observed, he had not changed a great deal in the intervening years. He was still a creature of society, basically frivolous in his pursuits and interests. She was quite unable to think of a single thing to say that might interest him, other than conventionally polite exchanges. As a result they spent a lot of their time together in silence. He was always courteous, but his boredom was palpable. It was small consolation that he was apparently as little impressed with all the other ladies—even the Season's successes—who tried to engage his attention, to flirt with him. He was much more charming with them, but he remained as elusive as ever.

Talk of *The Wicked Marquis*, which was widespread, was also a source of unease. She had read the novel herself of course, the night after receiving it from Lowell, and had been somewhat relieved. It was indeed very funny, and, apart from one or two shockingly salacious episodes, not nearly as scandalous as its cover would suggest. What was more, Lowell's additions and alterations had made it virtually impossible to guess the authorship from internal evidence. But everyone in London had identified Lord Baconwit, Beau Broombrain, and the rest, and quotations from it were free and frequent. And, though no respectable lady could admit to having read such a dreadful novel, there was much gossip and laughter at the expense of Hester's unfortunate victims.

After a while Hester stopped wincing inwardly when *The Wicked Marquis* came into the conversation, and was able to smile with the rest, feel indeed a faint touch of pride in its success. She was even willing to listen to Lowell's apologies.

Ten days after her arrival in London Hester came in, bored and tired from a shopping expedition, to find Lowell waiting for her. They were alone. Lady Perceval had gone up to her room.

'Hester! Look at this!'

Hester took the sheet he was holding out and carried it to the brighter light near the window. Though she had brought her grandfather's glasses with her, she never used them in public. She read out its contents with a sigh of rapture.

'"Mr Garimond announces a forthcoming Lecture to be given by an Eminent Cambridge Mathematician"—I wonder who that could be?—"under the Auspices of The New Scientific and Philosophical Society". Look, Lowell! Look! It's on my subject! "Algebra, Numbers and Ciphers—A New Approach". Where, where? And when?' Hester was so excited she could hardly speak. Lowell took the paper from her trembling hand.

'It's being given next Wednesday, at the Society's headquarters in St James's Street.'

'I must go!'

'Well…' Lowell looked uncomfortable. 'There's a problem.'

'What is it?'

'It's not an open lecture, Hes.'

'Not open? What does that mean?'

'The meeting is for gentlemen only. No ladies admitted.'

'But…but I must go!'

Lowell regretfully shook his head. 'It's not possible.'

Hester grew pale with rage and disappointment. 'Oh what a *devilish* world this is! I could explode, Lowell! The thought that you who are…are as ignorant as a swan in mathematics…'

'Steady on, Hester! I *can* count!'

His sister ignored this feeble interruption and swept on, 'You, who refuse even to *try* to understand ciphers, you can go freely among some of the best minds in England today, while I have to keep back and suffocate in the drawing-rooms of society… I shall burst with frustration!' She strode about the room, muttering, 'It's too bad! Too bad! Indeed, it is too bad!'

Lowell watched this display with some awe. He had long known his sister's views on the lack of opportunity for women, but this was the strongest demonstration yet. She looked magnificent in her rage, eyes flashing blue fire, cheeks glowing… He had seen for himself how Dungarran and the others dismissed his sister as quiet, insignificant and boring. If they could only see her now—a veritable tigress…

'Hester…' he said tentatively.

'No, Lowell! I'm not fit for company at the moment, and Mama might come in at any moment. Tell her I've gone upstairs to read, will you?'

'You…you won't do anything silly?'

'What is there to do? I might chew a few sheets, or tear up a few carpets, but nothing *serious*, such as going out without an escort or omitting to curtsey to Lady Jersey. But I wish to heaven you had not shown me that advertisement!' She went out.

Lowell also regretted his rash action. He had brought it without thinking of the consequences, only that Hester would be interested in the mention of Garimond and the Society. It was true that she was having a hard time in London. He was impressed at the effort she had made to please her parents. Only he knew how much she feared reminding the world of the cocksure girl she had been six years before, and of her subsequent humiliation. Only he knew the trouble she took to make unexceptionable conversation—but as soon as she was with someone who could be regarded as remotely eligible, she became quiet and dull. If only the world knew his sister as he did—teasing, laughing, affectionate, with a puckish sense of humour, and a strong liking for the ridiculous!

As he walked back to Half Moon Street that night he was deep in thought. The result was that he was back in Bruton Street the next day to invite Hester to a walk. She was pale and heavy-eyed, and responded reluctantly when Lady Perceval urged her to take the air. But eventually she and Lowell set off towards the park.

'I'm glad you came—I want to talk to you in private, Hes. I've had an idea, but I'm not sure you'll like it.'

'What is it?' asked Hester listlessly.

'You'd like to go to that lecture, wouldn't you?'

'Oh, don't talk any more of that! I couldn't sleep last night for thinking of it. But I can't go, and there's an end.'

'How much would you give to be able to attend?'

'Don't be so absurd! I can't *bribe* my way into an exclusively masculine meeting! I wouldn't feel comfortable if I did. Please don't mention it again, Lowell. It's too upsetting.'

'I wasn't thinking of money or bribes. Supposing you could disguise yourself?'

'Disguise myself? As what? A man? That's even more ridiculous! I would be discovered within seconds. And what a scandal *that* would cause!'

'No, you wouldn't! Hes, do think about it! It would be such a lark. You're tall enough for a man—a boy, anyway. You're thin enough. And Gaines left quite a bit of his stuff behind. Between us we could find something to fit you. No one would ever know.'

'I can't believe you mean it, Lowell! You're mad! It's far too risky! I wouldn't dream of doing such a thing.'

Lowell shrugged his shoulders. 'In that case, there's no more to be said.'

They walked on into the park. Hester was the first to break the silence. 'Besides, I don't even know where the Society's offices are.'

'We'd go together.'

'And what would I say to Mama?'

'Well, I suppose you could confess that you were going to a meeting for men only, disguised as a boy,' Lowell said with heavy irony. 'On the other hand, you could simply say that you were out for the evening with me. Look Hester, you could raise objections till the cows come home, but you know they could all be overcome with a little courage.'

'A little courage! My heavens, Lowell, you have no notion of what you're asking!'

'I'm not asking anything for me. It's you I was thinking of.'

'Don't try to tell me you wouldn't enjoy it, all the same. It's just the sort of mad escapade you love.'

'It'd be one in the eye for Hugo, too,' Lowell said with some satisfaction. 'He's so...so correct. Sir Hugely Perfect is just the right name for him. I always want to do something outrageous when he's been lecturing me.'

'In this case, it wouldn't be you, it would be me! And if you think I would risk my name and reputation just because you want to get even with Hugo you are very much mistaken, little brother! What has he been saying to you now?'

'Told me off for riding my horse,' Lowell said sulkily.

'You mean galloping at full stretch along Pall Mall for a wager? I heard about that. He was right.'

'Oh, not you too, Hes!'

Hester smiled, then grew serious. 'Do you...do you

really think we could get away with it? I would so love to go.'

'I'm sure of it.' Lowell's face brightened. 'Let's make a plan!'

Hester laughed. This had always been Lowell's favourite saying when he was about to embark on some reckless enterprise. Entering into the spirit of it, however, she demanded, 'Well then, what are the dangers?... My figure.'

'Hidden under coat, waistcoat and a well-arranged cravat.' Then he added with brotherly candour, 'Besides, there isn't much of it.'

Hester was too much a realist to be offended. 'My voice.'

'Deep enough, but you needn't use it. You'd be there to listen, not to talk.'

'What about my hair?'

'The front of your hair is short, anyway. We'll find something to do with the rest.'

'Admittance to the premises—under whose name?'

'They won't ask. But the subscription is in Gaines's name, so if they did we'd use that.'

Hester thought for a moment. 'It seems almost too easy,' she said slowly.

'Easy as falling off a log,' said Lowell. 'Trust me!'

'The last time you fell off a log you broke your collarbone. But... I think I will try it.'

The walkers in London's Hyde Park were suddenly startled by Lowell's jubilant 'Yoicks!'

Quite often during the ensuing days Hester wondered if she had gone mad. But then she reminded herself that she was about to enjoy a privilege normally denied to women, and her resolve held firm. She and Lowell held a dress rehearsal the day before the lecture, and when they had stopped laughing, she had to agree that she made a convincing youth, especially when Lowell produced her glasses and made her put them on.

'By Jupiter, Hes, you make a better-looking fellow than most of my friends!'

'You exaggerate. But I'm not bad.'

She stood admiring herself in the mirror. They had drawn her back hair into a knot, and hidden it under the inordinately high stand-up collar affected by young Mr Gaines. Her long legs were encased in yellow pantaloons, her upper half in a snowy shirt, an awesomely embroidered waistcoat and a starched, intricately folded cravat. Mr Gaines was inclined to dandyism, and her coat of blue superfine had handsome buttons, impressive lapels and well-padded shoulders.

'I hope it will be all right, Lowell,' she said suddenly. 'I don't like to think of the consequences if we're found out.'

'We shan't be. Remember what I've told you—lengthen your stride, don't talk at all unless you have to, and keep your voice deep if you do. We'll take care to stay at the back out of sight. We'll be as right as rain, you'll see. Unless Hugo comes.'

'Oh good God! I never thought of that! I can't do it!'

'Don't worry—he won't come,' Lowell said comfortably. 'He's taking Sophia Cleeve to Lady Sefton's soirée.'

'Then why did you say he might? Lowell, you are the world's worst tease!'

All went well the following evening. They were admitted without question to the Society's headquarters in St James's Street, though Lowell was asked to sign in an impressive-looking register. Then they followed others to a large room at the back. This had clearly been a ballroom when the house had been in private hands, but it was now used as a lecture hall, with rows of chairs, a platform at one end and a balcony at the other. Hester had to restrain herself from clutching Lowell's arm as they made their way to a seat at the back under the shelter of the overhanging balcony.

'Ideal!' whispered Lowell as they sat down. 'Now all you have to do is to keep mum.'

'I won't forget. But Lowell, what did you sign? You seemed to write two names. Gaines and what?'

Lowell looked uneasy. 'They asked if I had a pseudonym. So I put... I put your name.'

'*What?*'

'I wrote 'Euclid'. They were impressed. Don't worry! They were too busy to have a good look at us. Now hush, it's beginning. And remember! Not a word!'

The lecture that followed was all Hester could have wished. It confirmed what she already knew, it pre-

sented her with the result of others' researches, it gave
her food for a great deal of future speculation and
thought. And to be in such company, such an atmosphere, went to her head like champagne. She clapped
with enthusiasm when the speaker was thanked by Mr
Garimond, and when comments from the floor were
invited it was all she could do not to shower him with
questions. Remembering Lowell's warning, however,
she stayed in her seat. But then some nameless idiot
got up and dared to cast doubt on the usefulness or
purpose of substitute numbers, disparaging the study
of algebra and 'all that nonsense', and referring to the
whole field as toys for adults with no practical application. This was too much. Forgetting all caution, she
leapt up and demolished the pretentious arguments,
quoting the words of eminent mathematicians from
all ages, and pointing out the vital work of cryptog-
raphers in times of war. A round of applause greeted
her words and many turned to see this talented young
speaker.

Hester sat down to see Lowell staring at her in
consternation. He whispered, 'Of all the mutton-
headed things to do...! We'd better lope off as soon
as we can, otherwise we're for it. Look, the chair-
man's going to speak. We can slip out when all eyes
are on him.'

But it wasn't so easy. They had hardly got to the
end of the row when, after a brief conference on the
platform, Mr Garimond stood up.

'We believe the young man who has just spoken

to be one of our most gifted contributors. Am I right in thinking we have Euclid here? If so, our president, whom most of you know as Zeno, is eager to make his acquaintance.'

Hester stopped and turned, eager to see 'Zeno' at last. But to her dazed eyes the platform was filled with a tall, elegant figure. Dungarran, immaculate as ever, was standing at Garimond's side. 'No!' she whispered. 'No! He *can't* be!' She sat down suddenly in the empty chair at the end of the row. Dungarran appeared to be looking straight at her, and she cowered down behind the person in front.

Garimond went on, 'We should like young Euclid to come to the platform after these proceedings are over. And now…' He turned to other business.

Hester was still sitting in a daze when Lowell hauled her up by the sleeve. 'Come *on*, Hes! Unless you want to get caught here and now, we'd better get out. No one is looking at the moment. We can escape round the back of this pillar. Come *on*!'

Hester allowed herself to be dragged away. Her knees felt as if they were made of wax, and Lowell had to support her as they left the building. He spotted a hackney coach a few yards away and bundled her into it. They drove the short distance to Half Moon Street in silence. Having spoken so eloquently just a few minutes before Hester could not now say a word.

At Half Moon Street Lowell paid off the coachman, who cast a jaundiced eye over Hester and said gloomily, 'The lad's 'ad a bit too much from the look of 'im… Want any 'elp wiv cartin' 'im in?'

Lowell hastily refused and the coach drove off. Fortunately, Gaines's absence meant that there were fewer servants around to observe Lowell's efforts to get his sister safely hidden inside his room. It wasn't easy. Hester was still in a state of shock, and had to be led every inch of the way.

Once inside Lowell poured a glass of brandy and held it to her lips. She choked, and shuddered as the spirit went down, but it revived her.

'Lowell!' She took a deep breath. 'Lowell, I can't believe it!' she said, clutching his sleeve. 'Tell me it isn't true. Am I mad or was it indeed Dungarran on that platform?'

Lowell nodded slowly. 'I'm afraid he was, Hes.' He looked at her sympathetically. 'A bit of a shock, isn't it?'

Hester gave a gasping laugh. 'A *bit*! Dungarran as Zeno! It's impossible! He hasn't the brains.'

'Apparently he has.'

Hester felt as if her world had turned upside down. Her pride in her work, her delight in her exchanges with Zeno, her feeling of oneness with his mind—all these had been tossed into the air and now lay scattered around her. How could she reconcile all that with what she had learned tonight?

'Hes…' Lowell's voice seemed to come from a great distance. 'Hester, I don't want to worry you more than I have to, but it's time you went back to Bruton Street. Are you fit? Mama will be back soon.'

'Yes… Yes, of course.' She got up and went to the door.

'Wait! You can't go like that, Hester! What's wrong with you? You must change.'

'What? Oh, my clothes! Of course!' She looked round vaguely for her dress and the rest of her things.

'Are you sure you can manage?' Lowell looked so concerned that she made herself respond.

'Of course I can. Wait outside a minute or two. I'll call when I'm ready.'

Twenty minutes later Hester was back in the Bruton Street house. Her parents had not yet come in, and she was able to bid Lowell goodnight and go upstairs without encountering any of the family. Her maid exclaimed at the state of her hair, but Hester was too tired to listen, or to offer any explanation. In near silence she got ready for bed and when her mother came in she pretended to be asleep. The house gradually settled down for the night and Hester was left lying wide-eyed, alone with her thoughts.

They were not pleasant. She had learned to laugh both at herself and at those young men who had made her so unhappy six years before. It had taken time, but she had managed it. She had gradually forgotten the hurt and heartache they had caused, though her determination never to marry had remained undiminished. And, since coming to London again, she had found no reason to change her mind. She had comforted herself that she would go back to her attic when the Season was over and take up her secret work once again, her secret, totally satisfying relationship with a man called Zeno. She had basked in the knowledge that here was a man—however old, however distant—whom she admired, and who in turn admired her…

But tonight Dungarran, the heartless, shallow man of a frivolous society, someone whom she cordially disliked, for whom she certainly had little respect, had been revealed as Zeno, her hero and mentor. The world in which she had found such comfort, the world of the journal and Zeno, had been shattered. The only possible way to put the pieces back together again would be to change her view of Dungarran. Radically… The thought appalled her. She couldn't do it!

Her last and most despairing thought was that Zeno had been revealed as someone who knew Hester Perceval. Knew her already, and already despised her… Hester hid her face in her hands in despair.

Chapter Five

But as the night wore on hope started to grow once more. All was not lost. As long as Robert Dungarran remained ignorant of Euclid's identity, she and Zeno could continue their work together. It would not be easy to reconcile Dungarran, the indolent man of fashion and one of her cruellest critics, with the figure of Zeno, the serious mathematician and her treasured friend. But, if she were strong-minded enough, she could derive some ironic amusement from the situation—the respect Zeno and Euclid had for each other contrasted with the dislike and contempt felt between Robert Dungarran and Hester Perceval. Yes! It could work. That was how she would regard it—as a piquant, amusing situation. She must, if she were to survive.

By the time Friday dawned, Hester was, on the surface at least, almost her normal self again. When she found that her glasses were missing, she concluded that she had probably left them in her brother's rooms on the night of the lecture, and walked quite cheerfully round to Half Moon Street. It was, in any case, time to have a talk with Lowell.

Lowell was in, and glad to see her. 'I called at Bruton Street yesterday to see how you were. But the house was deserted.'

'We spent half the day with Aunt Elizabeth. Have you seen my glasses? I must have left them somewhere here the other night.' As they rummaged among the piles of books and newspapers she went on, 'You know, I think London has done Robina a lot of good. She's such a pretty thing, and now she actually appears to be coming out of her shell.'

'Good for her! Aunt Elizabeth is far too strict with all the girls!'

'If only she weren't such a perfectionist! Poor Robina is forever afraid of failing to live up to her mother's expectations. Ah! here they are!' She picked up her glasses and put them on without thinking. She continued, 'It's not that Aunt Elizabeth is unkind. Not at all. Did you know that she's thinking of inviting poor Deborah Staunton to live with them in Abbot Quincey?'

'Deborah! At the Vicarage! For God's sake, don't tell Hugo! He'd never come home if he heard that.' They both grinned. Lady Elizabeth's niece Deborah had a genius for getting into scrapes, and Hugo had been involved in one or two of them a couple of years back. He still hadn't forgiven her. He had sworn at the time that he would never come within a mile of the girl again! There was a short silence, then Hester said, 'Lowell, I've been thinking…'

Lowell instantly grew serious. 'About Dungarran?'

'Yes. I couldn't see straight on Wednesday night, but now I've had a chance to think it over. If we can only keep him from finding out that I'm Euclid, there's nothing to stop us carrying on as before. Is there?'

Lowell thought. 'You mean writing for the journal and the rest? I suppose not,' he said slowly. 'And it shouldn't be all that difficult to keep Euclid's identity a secret. Dungarran is most unlikely to spend a lot of time finding him, it's not his style. Besides, how could he do it? The only clue he might have is Gaines's name from the register, and Gaines is safely tucked away in Devon for the summer. He would have to go to some trouble to find out this address, and I can't see him doing that—it can't be all that important. No, Hes, I think you're safe.'

At that moment they heard a knock on the street door and a murmured discussion. A minute later the servant came to ask if Mr Perceval would see Lord Dungarran.

Hester looked at Lowell in consternation, and shook her head imploringly. But Lowell knew better. It was impossible to deny such an important visitor, impossible even to keep him waiting.

'Show Lord Dungarran in, Withers.' Then he turned to Hester and said rapidly, 'Be as female as you can, Hes. High voice, fluttery manner—you know! And for goodness' sake, take your glasses off!' Hester snatched off her spectacles just as Dungarran strolled in, ducking slightly as he came through the low door.

'Good afternoon, Perceval. I hope you don't mind my calling like this without warning.'

'Not at all, not at all,' said Lowell with a fair degree of calm. 'I believe you know my sister, sir.'

'Miss Perceval! Forgive me, I didn't see you there in the shadows. How d'y do?'

They exchanged the usual greeting and enquiries. Hester knew that, in common courtesy, she should offer to leave the gentlemen to it. But she was determined to stay. She sat down firmly by the window and smiled sweetly. 'Pay no attention to me,' she said airily. 'I shall return to Bruton Street in a few minutes, but meanwhile I shall sit here and gather my strength. The weather is so fatiguing, do you not think, Lord Dungarran? My brother was just about to offer me some lemonade. Weren't you, Lowell?'

'Why…y…yes!' Lowell put his head out of the door and talked to Withers.

Dungarran walked over to the bookcase and examined the titles there. Hester regarded him from her vantage point by the window. He looked his usual, calmly superior self, and yet how differently she now saw him! Somewhere behind that lazily fashionable façade, was Zeno, her respected ally and friend, a man whose mind she knew better than anyone else's. She savoured the notion. The feeling that she knew more about Robert Dungarran than he knew of her was strangely heady!

Dungarran cleared his throat and turned. 'Were you

with Hugo and Lady Sophia at Lady Sefton's soirée, Miss Perceval?'

'Last Wednesday? No. I was otherwise engaged.' Amusement threatened to bubble to the surface. It was hard not to laugh. What would the gentleman say if she told him where she had in fact been?

'Ah!'

With a touch of audacity she asked, 'Why? Were you, Lord Dungarran?'

'No. I too, had a previous engagement.' He turned as Lowell came back. 'Ah, Perceval!'

'Now, how can I serve you, sir?' Lowell cleared one of the chairs by the simple expedient of throwing a pile of journals to the floor. 'Do, pray, take a seat.'

Dungarran sat down. There was a pause. Then he began. 'I have to say I was surprised to find you in possession here, Perceval. I thought to meet a Mr Gaines—a Mr Woodford Gaines.'

The servant came in with some cool drinks. When he went out Lowell said casually, 'The house does belong to Gaines, yes, but he recently left London…'

'*Very* recently,' said Hester, giving Lowell a significant look.

Lowell nodded. 'Very recently. He lets me have rooms here, and for the moment I'm the sole tenant. Do you know Gaines?'

'Not…exactly. I thought I saw him with you the other night.'

'Saw me? Where?'

'At a lecture on mathematics.'

There was a small noise as Hester's glasses slithered to the floor. Dungarran rose from his chair and gathered them up.

'You're lucky, Miss Perceval. They don't appear to be broken.'

'Oh…oh, thank you, but they're not mine, sir!' she said nervously. 'I must have picked them off the seat. Are they yours, Lowell?'

Lowell rose nobly to the occasion. 'They might belong to Gaines.' Then he turned to his visitor. 'I'm sorry, no, I wasn't with Gaines on Wednesday evening. I was with my sister.' He laughed. 'A lecture on mathematics would be the last place my friends would expect to find me!' His sister looked at him sharply. Lowell, too, was enjoying this game, but she hoped he wouldn't overplay it. He went on, 'But why do you ask?'

Dungarran smiled lazily. That smile, thought Hester viewing it objectively, might well charm an unwary bird out of a tree—but the bird might end up feeling it had made a mistake. 'I'm sorry. You must think me impertinent. At the risk of boring you, I should like to explain. I have a…slight interest in mathematics myself, and for some time now I've been in correspondence with a gifted mathematician, someone whom I only know as Euclid…'

He went on to give them an account, which they didn't need, of the events on the evening of the lecture. 'And now I am at a loss. The young gentleman in question did not turn up at the end as I had hoped. I rather thought I had tracked him down when I traced him to this address. Tell me, how long is Mr Gaines likely to be out of London?'

'Till the autumn.'

'Ah.'

Greatly daring, Hester asked, 'May I ask why you are so anxious to meet this…Eugene?'

'Euclid, Miss Perceval. Euclid. He was an eminent mathematician in ancient times.'

Hester opened her eyes wide. 'Mr *Gaines* was? I don't understand.'

'Why should you?' Dungarran smiled indulgently. 'The journal for which both he and I write has the rather bizarre custom of giving its contributors pseudonyms from the past—'

'Do you mean to tell me that you actually *write*, Lord Dungarran? For a journal?'

'Pray do not disturb yourself, ma'am. I do not permit my work to interfere with my social commitments.'

'So I have observed. But what do you write?' she asked ingenuously. 'Poetry?'

'Not exactly.' He turned to Lowell. 'I should very much like to meet the fellow. Though he appears to be very young, he is extremely talented. There are aspects of his work which interest me greatly. Are you quite certain that you cannot help me?'

Lowell spread his hands regretfully. 'I'm afraid I can't,' he said. 'Gaines is in Devon on a walking tour with his godfather. I've no idea where is at the moment, only that he will be back in the autumn.'

'Ah. That's a pity. Then I apologise for wasting

your time. I'll finish up this very good ale and then go. May I escort you home, Miss Perceval?'

'Thank you, sir, but my footman is waiting outside,' said Hester, not without a certain satisfaction.

He nodded in approval, sat back and took another draft of his beer. Still looking into the glass, he said casually, 'So you're not a mathematician?' and followed this with a quick glance at Lowell from grey eyes which were unusually keen.

'Far from it!' exclaimed Lowell. 'I was never so glad in all my life when the time came to put my primers away for good.'

Dungarran nodded. 'A heartfelt reaction—and one most people share. That's why I keep rather quiet about my own fascination with the subject. Few wish to hear about the application of algebra, or the new research into calculus.'

'Calculus?' Hester asked sharply. Lowell and Dungarran looked at her in astonishment. She gave a little laugh and faltered, 'Oh, you must excuse me! My mind was wandering. Were you talking about another of your friends? Like Eugene? Was Calculus at the lecture, too?'

'Er...no. Just Euclid. But we must be boring you, Miss Perceval. Forgive me.'

Hester bit back the protest which rose to her lips, gave a bell-like laugh and said, 'It would be rude of me to confess to being bored! But I daresay many ladies would have better uses for a ballroom than holding a lecture on mathematics in it!'

Dungarran looked at her thoughtfully, then smiled

and got up to go. 'I'm sure you are right! And if you don't need my company to Bruton Street, I'll take my leave.' He bowed, then turned to Lowell. 'Should you hear anything from the mysterious Mr Gaines, Perceval, I'd be obliged if you ask him to get in touch with me.'

He went out. Lowell breathed a deep sigh of relief. Hester frowned and said thoughtfully, 'All the same, Lowell…'

'Well?'

'All the same, if I were you I would prepare a very good reason for being at that lecture. Dungarran, I can assure you, is far from stupid. I don't think he was completely convinced by your evasions.'

'What nonsense! Why on earth should he think I'd go to a lecture on mathematics, of all things?'

'That's what you must think out for yourself!'

'Unnecessary, my dear sister. You wait and see— it will be quite unnecessary!'

Lowell would not have been quite so sure of himself if he could have seen into their recent visitor's mind as he walked back to Curzon Street. Dungarran was quite certain that Lowell Perceval had been at the lecture. How else would Hester Perceval have known that it had been held in a former ballroom? Obviously because her brother had mentioned the ballroom in the St James's Street house when he had told her about the lecture. He had also let slip that he knew when it was held. Interesting. Young Mr Perceval had enjoyed playing with him! That would account for the air of suppressed amusement about both the Percevals which had so intrigued him. Still deep in thought, he entered his house, handed his hat and cane to the footman waiting at the door, and sent for his man.

'Ah, Wicklow. Good. Come through to the library and shut the door, will you?'

It would be difficult to describe Wicklow's exact role in the Dungarran household. He was his lordship's manservant, everyone knew that. Indeed, he was the very epitome of a gentleman's gentleman. Neat as a pin himself, with a thin, pale, somewhat melancholy face, quietly discreet in his movements, he looked after Dungarran's wardrobe with consummate skill. But he had other functions connected with his master's less well-known activities, and it was for this work he was now needed.

'Wicklow, you were prompt in finding Mr Woodford Gaines's address. Did you learn anything else about him?'

'Not much, my lord. He appeared to be a perfectly normal young man. A bit of a dandy, they said. Your lordship asked for speed and discretion in the matter, so I did not spend more time than necessary with his associates.'

'Quite right, quite right. You did well. But now I want you—still with discretion—to establish two things. Mr Gaines left London recently, possibly for Devon. I want you to find out first exactly when he left, and second exactly where he went—Devon, or anywhere else. And Wicklow!'

Wicklow, who had been about to leave the room, turned and waited.

'I would prefer you to avoid annoying Mr Lowell Perceval with your enquiries. You will obviously not approach Mr Perceval's sister, either. Thank you, that is all.'

After Wicklow had gone Dungarran sat in silence reviewing his conversation with the two Percevals. He had seen from the outset that they were very close, and he rather thought that Lowell would confide fairly freely in his sister. They had been quite good, those two. Only two slips—one by Lowell, one by his sister. He smiled grimly at the neat way in which Master Lowell had ostensibly denied having been at the lecture, without actually lying. 'A lecture on mathematics would be the last place my friends would expect to find me.' Very neat. But why avoid that lie when he had told one already? 'I was with my sister.' And why say it with such amusement? If he *had* been at the lecture he could not possibly have been with his sister. There was no doubt that Hester Perceval would support anything her brother said, but why had he felt the alibi necessary? It might be odd that Lowell Perceval should wish to attend a lecture on mathematics, but there was nothing *wrong* with it… Unless there was something suspicious about Gaines himself…?

Where the devil was Euclid? Why had he vanished from the Society's rooms last Wednesday, and why had he left London immediately afterwards? Robert Dungarran got up and walked about the room restlessly… Perhaps they were all wasting his time—it wasn't certain that Gaines and Euclid were one and the same person. The signature in the register was no real proof. Had Lowell Perceval signed it, using Gaines's name…? As a wager, perhaps? Lowell Perceval was known for his mad escapades. He gave a gesture of impatience. There were too many questions. He would have to wait till Wicklow found some answers. Meanwhile, there was work to be done… Dungarran went to the handsome desk in a corner of the room and took out some papers.

But after a moment he sat back with a sigh of exasperation. The situation was absurd. Buried in the papers, which had been removed with great difficulty from Napoleon's headquarters in Paris and brought to England at considerable risk, there could be vital background information about the food and weapons situation in France and the army's lines of supply. But they were all in cipher. If they were to be useful to the Allies then they would have to be transcribed before very long. The War Office would soon get impatient. He needed help, and Euclid, with his outstanding talent for ciphers and the speed with which he worked, was the very man. And now the wretch had become elusive! It was to be hoped that Wicklow would find him…

But the result of Wicklow's investigations only raised more questions. Mr Woodford Gaines had left London for Totnes in Devon on 15 April—two weeks before the lecture ever took place. He had not been seen in Half Moon Street since then, and was generally assumed to be walking in the Dart valley with a godfather of whom he had great expectations. There were no other inhabitants of the Half Moon Street house, and Mr Perceval's other close friends had all been at a reunion.

So who was the second young gentleman who had been in St James's Street with Lowell Perceval? Where was he?

Over the next few days Dungarran pondered this mystery. It had become important to him to solve it— and not just to satisfy his curiosity. He had had confidence in Euclid. The correspondence with the fellow had given him a great deal of pleasure. It was rare to find a mind so much in harmony with his own, and all his instincts had been to trust him. Whether Euclid realised it or not, he had been deciphering bits of foreign documents for some time now—aiding and confirming Dungarran's own work for the government. Any mystery about him was most unwelcome.

He decided to investigate from another starting point—the collection and delivery of Euclid's contributions—and went round to the Society's headquarters to question the staff himself. The day porter at the entrance was old and half blind, and only vaguely remembered receiving and handing out various sealed papers over the months. He provided a description of the agent which could fit Lowell Perceval—and a hundred others as well. The junior porter's description of the young man who had signed the register on the evening of the lecture, however, could hardly be anyone else.

'Yes, I remember 'im, my lord. A very 'andsome young gentleman. Young, tall, wiv fair 'air and blue eyes. Looks as if 'e's laughin' all the time…'

When questioned about any other young gentleman, the porter was less certain. 'There was someone else… But whether 'e was wiv the first young gentleman, I couldn't rightly swear to… Very shy, 'e was—kept in the background. One thing I do remember—'e wore glasses. I didn't see nothink else. Oh!' He pocketed the coin, Dungarran had handed him. 'Your lordship's very kind. I'm sorry I can't 'elp you more.'

Things seemed to have reached an impasse. He decided to consult someone whose good sense and intelligence he considered as good, if not better than his own. He betook himself to his aunt. Lady Martindale was a childless widow and lived alone in a large house in Grosvenor Street. She had been the late Lady Dungarran's favourite sister, and was Robert Dungarran's godmother. They were frequently seen together. Society knew that Lady Martindale was very attached to her nephew, but most would have been astonished to learn how highly the nephew thought of her intelligence and discretion, and how much he confided in her. She was one of the few people in London who knew of his activities at the Foreign Office. Her husband had been a diplomat, and it was through his persuasion that Dungarran had taken up his work there.

'I have a problem, Godmama—' he began.

'You seldom come unless you have, Robert. What is it this time? Could it possibly be a woman?'

Dungarran smiled. 'You never give up, do you? Why do you doubt my ability to manage my own love affairs?'

'Love affairs, indeed!' Lady Martindale gave an unladylike snort. 'You don't know what love means! You mean flirtations, or liaisons with ladies of more beauty than virtue—that doesn't mean love to me!'

'Whatever you say, dearest. I won't argue,' he said indifferently. But she was not to be put off.

'You've been spoilt, my boy! Ever since you came of age women—of every kind—have found you fascinating—'

Dungarran made a face. 'Please! We both know that any rich, reasonably personable man would interest the ladies, don't we?'

'That may be so. But it is a fact that when you exert yourself you usually find most women responsive. And that isn't good for you.'

This frank speaking was not to her godson's taste. 'You make me out to be a veritable coxcomb, Aunt,' he said somewhat coolly. 'As far as I know, I have never raised false hopes in any female breast. Except perhaps once...' he stopped. 'No matter.'

His godmother waited hopefully, but it became clear he was not going to amplify. She took up her theme again. 'When you do fall in love, Robert—and I hope I may live to see it—you might not have such an easy time. Things don't always go as we plan when the heart is involved. You might be glad of a shoulder to cry on then.'

'Let us not get into the realms of fantasy, Aunt Martindale,' he said impatiently. 'It is highly unlikely, if not impossible, that my heart would ever rule my head to such an irrational extent. I'm surprised at you. I thought you had more sense.'

Lady Martindale shook her head. 'Stronger men than you have fallen, Robert.'

'But not, I think, more logical ones. Now, may I consult you on a certain problem, or are we to carry on spinning fairy tales?'

'What is it?' she asked in a resigned tone.

He had no need to tell her of his correspondence with Euclid, or of his work on ciphers. She knew all this. So he briefly related the puzzling events of the night of the lecture, and the information he had since gathered. She requested him to repeat his account of the meeting with the Percevals in Half Moon Street, and asked one or two questions. At the end she said slowly, 'Why are you so sure that Euclid is a man?'

He looked at her in surprise. 'What else could he be? There are no women in this case.'

'Oh, come, Robert! You are not usually so stupid! There is one at least!'

'You mean Hester Perceval?' He began to smile. 'You've met her?'

'I've seen her. But I haven't spoken to her.'

'Well!' He looked at her as if he had said enough. When she continued to look at him in silence, he went on, 'Godmama, Euclid is a man of the quickest wits, and a penetrating mind. He has a very good feeling for mathematics and has an instinct for finding the key to difficult ciphers which almost amounts to genius.'

'So?'

'What is more, he has a sense of humour, an appreciation of the ridiculous, which is very like my own. You've seen Hester Perceval. How can you possibly think that she could be Euclid?'

'Why not?'

'She…she's dull! She's…she's… Well, that's it, really. She's dull. Boring.' Lady Martindale was still silent. 'Look,' he said in exasperation. 'Euclid has the flexibility of mind that all the great decipherers have. Hester Perceval is as rigid, as fixed in her ideas as a woman can be. Did you know her six years ago?'

'No, I didn't. Your uncle and I came late to London that year. And she left halfway through, after that business with Canford. I heard about her, of course.'

'You must have been told how she came to town with a mission, ignoring all advice and insisting on spreading her half-baked theories, learned by heart from her schoolteacher's preachings. She was supposed to have been a prize pupil, but, I assure you, there was little indication of cleverness in her dealings with the world! We all were heartily sick of her.'

'Robert, she cannot have been very old. What was she—seventeen? Eighteen? I feel sorry for the girl.'

'So was I. But I was even sorrier for her family, I assure you. And I think I may safely say that she hasn't changed much. Six years later she may be quieter, but in all our meetings she has not uttered a single original thought. Hester Perceval as Euclid? Impossible.' He got up and walked about the room. 'Impossible!'

'I don't think I can help, then. As far as I can see, there doesn't seem to be any other candidate for Euclid.' She looked at him, with a slight frown. 'You are usually very open-minded. But you seem to have a very strong prejudice against Miss Perceval. Are you quite sure she is as stupid as you say? Have you paid particular attention to her since she has come back?'

'I haven't dared,' he muttered.

'Aha! So she's the one...' He looked faintly exasperated as she smiled at him. 'Six years ago she thought she was in love with you, is that it? Don't be so conceited, Robert. Six years is a long time for a girl to hold on to an unrequited passion.'

'Hester Perceval cordially dislikes me, Godmama. So much is perfectly clear.'

'In that case, where is the danger? But you may observe her from a safe distance. She just might surprise you.'

'I doubt that very much. But since I still haven't yet finished with her brother, I may see something new. They might well be at tonight's reception at Carlton House.'

'Are you still free to take me?'

'Of course! What makes you think I might not?'

'I heard about the state they're in at the Horse Guards about those papers...'

'My dear godmother, they're always in a state at the Horse Guards! I'm about to go to work on their confounded papers, but there's this business of Euclid to settle first. We'll forget the Horse Guards this evening and enjoy ourselves—as long as we can keep our distance from Bathurst and his minions.'

'Let's hope the wine at Carlton House is better than it was the last time we dined there!'

After the concert Dungarran observed the Perceval family making its way into the Long Gallery. He decided to make use of the occasion. 'Aunt, you said you haven't been introduced to Miss Perceval...'

'I've met the senior Percevals, and I know Hugo, of course, very well. But not the two younger ones. Do you mean to introduce us?'

'I'd like to. As you know, I want to have a further word with Lowell Perceval, and this seems a good opportunity.'

'I'm disappointed. I hoped you wanted me to meet the young lady.'

Dungarran pulled a face. 'Hester Perceval is not my kind of young lady.'

'You must tell me some time what is, Robert,' sighed his godmother, as she followed him through the crowd. It was an ambition of hers to see her nephew settled, but as time went on she was growing less and less optimistic. It was not for want of opportunity. Over the years she had observed more than one accredited beauty fluttering her wings in his direction. But though he gave every sign of being

charmed, he had never succumbed. Even now, as they
greeted their acquaintances on the way through to the
Perceval family, she was amused by the many lan-
guishing glances cast by ladies who should have
known better. It was not only his handsome face and
tall figure which women found attractive, she thought.
He had an air of detachment which most women
found an irresistible challenge. She smiled. If they
only knew its origin! Robert had had his fair share of
mistresses, but when it came down to it he was far
more interested in the mysteries of mathematics than
the mysteries of love! Too well bred to show complete indifference in society, he was nevertheless
bored by most social exchanges. What sort of woman
would it take, she wondered, to break through that
barrier? Not one of your conventional society beau-
ties, that was certain!

They had reached the Percevals. She greeted the
parents with a friendly smile, and exchanged a few
words with Hugo. Then Robert said, 'Aunt, I'd like
to introduce Miss Hester Perceval…and Mr Lowell
Perceval.' The lady curtsied, the young man—and
what a personable young man he was!—bowed.

She studied them with interest, while Robert joined
in general talk with the family. At first sight it seemed
that all the good looks in the family had gone to the
male line. Hester Perceval was almost as tall as her
brother—too tall, perhaps, for a woman. She was
rather thin, and fashionably but quietly dressed in a
pale muslin evening dress with a somewhat limp fall
of lace round the neckline. Her hair was fair like that

of her brothers, but its natural curls were smoothed
down at the front and drawn into neat bands behind.
If the girl had set out to make herself as dull and
inconspicuous as possible, she could not have done
better! Her brother, on the other hand, was every bit
as good-looking as Hugo, but with a more immediately charming manner. In contrast to Hugo's air of
calm assurance, there was a reckless air about him,
and laughter seemed to hover round his mobile mouth
and deep blue eyes. He was still young—younger,
perhaps, than his years—but when he once grew up…
A real charmer, though essentially a lightweight
young man. It was obvious that the two younger
Percevals were devoted to each other, though she suspected that the sister had the stronger character.

When Hugo and Sir James and Lady Perceval
started to move off Lady Martindale took a step back,
but Robert gave a slight shake of his head and looked
briefly in the direction of Miss Perceval. Lady
Martindale was as quick as the next woman at taking
a hint.

Chapter Six

'I hear you come from Northamptonshire,' Lady Martindale said, turning back to Hester. 'Tell me, do you know Lord Yardley and his delightful family? I don't believe I saw you at the ball the Yardleys gave for their daughter's come-out. That was a splendid affair...' For the next few minutes she chatted with the sister while Robert held the brother in conversation. Hester Perceval was polite, if rather colourless in her manner. But she was noticeably uneasy. She kept looking towards the two men as if anxious to know what they were saying, and her sigh of relief when they turned back to the ladies was almost audible.

Lowell Perceval was looking ruefully guilty, rather like a small boy caught out in some mischief.

'Hester, I'm afraid it's all up! Lord Dungarran has flushed me out. I've had to confess that I was at the lecture the other night.'

'I am surprised Lord Dungarran is so interested,' said Hester coolly.

'I hate mysteries, Miss Perceval,' said Dungarran with one of his charming smiles. His aunt's interest quickened. Robert was dangerous when he smiled like this.

'What is mysterious about my brother's attendance at a lecture?'

Lady Martindale decided to take a part. 'A mystery? A lecture? Robert, what is all this about?'

'I'm sorry, Aunt. I'm being very rude. Forgive me. Mr Perceval was at a lecture at the Society last Wednesday, and when I quite mistakenly thought he was denying it, I was puzzled—and, yes, a little put out, too. It was one of the best I've heard.'

'I see. But where is the mystery in that?'

'Mr Perceval claims he has no interest in mathematics. So what puzzles me is why he was there at all!'

For a moment Lowell looked at a loss, and the girl next to Lady Martindale stiffened. Then she said with a laugh, 'I can see you're going to have to tell them about your wagers, Lowell!' She turned to Lady Martindale, and with the first sign of vivacity she had shown she said, 'You must know, Lady Martindale, that my brother cannot resist a wager. Have you heard of his exploits in Piccadilly?' She went on to explain in some detail how Lowell had ridden his horse at full gallop down one of London's main thoroughfares. She omitted no detail, describing the horses he had startled, the wagons he had narrowly missed, the carriages, the personages... Lady Martindale listened while she watched her nephew from the corner of her eye. Miss Perceval was making a brave effort to distract attention from the subject of Lowell's attendance at the lecture, but Robert, she knew, would not be put off. For all his relaxed air of someone who is enjoying an amusing anecdote, he was only waiting for the end of the recital to repeat his original question.

When Hester finally ran out of breath, he said, 'And all without real injury to anyone! You must be quite an accomplished horseman, Perceval! But what sort of a wager could entice you into the lair of the New Scientific and Philosophical Society?'

Lowell once again hesitated, and his sister once again came to his rescue.

'It was probably because of something I said, Lord Dungarran. I…er… I could not believe that Lowell would survive a lecture on such an uninteresting subject for more than half an hour. Oh! Forgive me, I mean no offence. I merely meant that it seems a dull subject to those who do not understand it.' She paused. 'To those who do, I am sure it is fascinating.' Her words were innocent enough, and the tone was obviously meant to convey that Miss Perceval was not to be counted among them. But Lady Martindale sensed something more than this about it. Was it irony? Or mockery? There was certainly a thread of amusement. She looked at her nephew, but he appeared not to have noticed. His eyes were on Lowell Perceval.

He said with a smile, 'And was it such a penance? The young man who was with you seemed to be an enthusiast. I have seldom heard such impassioned words in defence of the subject! It can't have been Mr Gaines, surely?'

Mr Perceval was now on his guard. 'Why not?' he asked warily.

'You told me yourself. He's in Devon with his god-father. And someone told me—can that have been you, too?—that he left London well before that Wednesday evening.'

The two Percevals exchanged glances. Lady Martindale was now in complete agreement with her nephew. These two were playing some game of their own. She could see that Robert was intent on challenging them. There was steel behind the amusement in his voice, and he did not take his eyes from Lowell's.

'Lowell! That's too bad of you!' Hester's exasperated exclamation cut into the pause. 'My wager was that you should go alone, without other distractions. If you had the company of another young man to keep you amused, then I consider that you have lost!'

'Lord Dungarran is mistaken, Hester, I swear. I wasn't with another man! It's true that someone next to me made a speech. He seemed to get a bit burned up, but I thought the whole thing very boring. You still owe me.'

Two pairs of eyes turned to Dungarran. Lady Martindale could see Hester's clearly for the first time. They were as deep a blue as those of her brother, and had the same limpidly innocent look in them. Her mouth twitched as she heard her nephew say, 'So you cannot help me, after all. How very annoying! I shall have to think again.'

And she wondered if the Percevals were as little deceived as she was by these words. They might well be congratulating themselves on winning the first round in this war of wits, but she would venture a considerable sum on her nephew to win the match—and, unlike the Percevals' so-called wager, the bet would be genuine!

Lady Martindale had derived considerable amusement from witnessing this exchange. She had no doubt that her nephew would be the victor in any battle of wits, but she suspected that he had at last met a worthy opponent—and not in the person of Lowell Perceval! She spent the next week or two watching the young Percevals closely and found nothing to cause her to change her mind. Hester Perceval was an enigma. When she said as much to her nephew he laughed at her.

'My dear aunt! In what way can Hester Perceval possibly interest you? What on earth is enigmatic about her?'

'You are very scornful of Miss Perceval, Robert. But in my view she must be unique! Young ladies enjoying a Season in London usually take endless pains with their appearance. Every skill known to their mamas, their dressmakers and their maids is employed to enhance their charms.'

'With varying success,' said Robert with a grin. 'And in Miss Perceval's case, very little.'

'But that's just it! She doesn't try for success, Robert! That is what makes her unique! I have never before met a girl who appears to make every effort not to *improve*, but to minimise her looks.'

'Oh, come! That cannot be so.'

'I mean it! Her aim seems to be to disappear into the background. Her manners are well-bred, but they lack any personality. Her clothing is so un-noteworthy that five minutes after leaving her one has difficulty in remembering what she was wearing—'

'But that's because she is a very dull girl!'

'You think so? I don't believe I can agree with you. It surely did not escape you that it was the sister, not the brother, who found the excuses for Lowell's behaviour at your famous lecture? And I suspect she put herself forward in a most uncharacteristic manner to do so.'

'So you didn't believe in Lowell's reasons any more than I did?'

'No. But did you not notice that it was Hester's quick-wittedness which saved him each time?'

'And frustrated me.' He thought for a moment. 'I must confess I was concentrating on the young man. I didn't notice his sister's efforts. Are you sure it was so?'

'Yes, Robert!' said Lady Martindale firmly. 'And if you have not seen Miss Perceval when she is unaware of being watched, then I have. She is a different creature altogether. Altogether livelier and much more attractive.'

Robert Dungarran's tone revealed his continuing

scepticism. 'I cannot claim to have watched her as assiduously as you apparently have, but in my experience Hester Perceval could be described as neither quick-witted nor lively, and, though I'm sorry for the girl, I simply cannot imagine she could ever be attractive!'

'You belong to the wrong group of people, my boy! With Lowell Perceval's friends, where she is perfectly at ease, she is a delightful creature—she laughs and teases, and is clearly popular with them all. It is only when she comes into Society with a capital ''S'' that she is suddenly subdued.'

'You're imagining things!'

'I assure you I am not! As soon as Hester Perceval comes into contact with anyone who could be described as ''eligible'' she freezes. I have seen her!'

'Then why else is she in London?'

'I have heard that she is here most unwillingly. Her parents more or less insisted on it.'

He was silent for a moment. Then he said, 'It would not be surprising if the poor girl was reluctant to venture into society again. Her first attempt ended in disaster... And if she finds amusement with Lowell Perceval and his friends then I am glad for her, though I am surprised. They seem very immature with their tricks and wagers. But my dear aunt, let us now talk of something else. I confess that I still find Miss Perceval a very boring topic of conversation!'

Lady Martindale gave up and talked of other matters. But she did not change her mind about Hester Perceval, and unobtrusively cultivated the girl's acquaintance. To this end she invited the Perceval family to one of her dinner parties.

She invited her nephew, too, and though he was still preoccupied with his translation of the French documents, he agreed to come. He was less than pleased, however, when he discovered that his partner for the evening was Hester Perceval. But since his manners were impeccable, apart from casting a speaking glance at his aunt, he saw Miss Perceval to her place and sat down beside her with every appearance of pleasure. There was a short silence while he considered what the devil he should say to the girl.

'Are you enjoying your stay in London, Miss Perceval?' he finally asked.

She looked at him thoughtfully as if debating what to reply. He wondered irritably what on earth the problem was. Surely a purely conventional 'Very much!' or 'Naturally' or even a noncommital 'Sometimes' would do? Then they could safely go on to discuss the latest balls and concerts. That should last through several courses.

'I didn't at first, Lord Dungarran. But now I am enjoying myself very much.' He was so surprised at this that he threw her a quick glance. She looked down immediately, but not before he had caught a hint of mischief in the blue depths of her eyes.

'Oh? Why is that?'

'I... I have discovered that an old friend of mine is here,' she said demurely. 'Someone I have known for several years, but have not till now met in person.'

'Ah! Do I sense a romance?'

'Oh no! Nothing like that. Our friendship is based on a meeting of minds. But it is very…interesting, nonetheless, to meet him.'

Dungarran nodded but sighed inwardly. He was doubtless about to hear of some worthy lady or elderly gentleman from the north, a missionary, or a reformer or something of that sort. He braced himself for a dissertation on the virtues of some undoubtedly very boring person.

'I don't suppose I know him, do I?'

'He is not known to society in general,' she said somewhat evasively. 'His talents are not ones which are commonly valued by the Ton.'

It was as he had thought. A preacher, or possibly one of the new radical thinkers, earnest in manner and depressingly dull in appearance. He persevered. 'And are you happy with your new acquaintance? Are his appearance and conversation as you imagined them?'

'They are radically different! In fact, I even occasionally find myself disliking him. But then I remember my former admiration and then…' She shook her head. 'To tell the truth, I am not yet sure what I think of him. It is…most interesting.' She glanced at him, and he was once again surprised by a gleam of amusement, mockery almost, in her eyes. What the devil was Miss Perceval up to? Her eyes were lowered again as she asked, 'But may I ask if you have yet traced your elusive mathematician?'

There was no doubt this time. Miss Perceval's manner was conventionally polite, the question harmless enough, but Robert Dungarran was nobody's fool. All his instincts—instincts which had served him well in the past—confirmed his suspicion that Miss Perceval was somehow making fun of him. A most unaccustomed flick of temper gave his next words unusual sharpness.

'Not yet. But I will.' His eyes rested for a moment on Lowell, seated further down the table. 'And I am quite certain that your brother knows more about Euclid than he will admit, Miss Perceval.' Keen grey eyes locked on to hers. 'Moreover, I strongly suspect that you are in his confidence. Am I right?'

Her eyes did not waver as she stared calmly back at him. 'Are you suggesting that my brother is Euclid? I assure you that he is as ignorant as a swan on mathematical matters.'

'I accept your word for that. Besides, it agrees with what I have discovered. Your brother's talents did not lie in the sciences in Cambridge. I am sure, however, that he knows Euclid, and was with him at that lecture. The signatures in the register for the evening are both in his handwriting.'

There was a pause. Then she said with not the slightest trace of amusement in her voice, 'I do not quite understand why you are pursuing the question of Euclid's identity with such determination, Lord Dungarran. But if you think Lowell knows more about Euclid than he has admitted, then you must talk to him—at another time, perhaps. I do not think Lady Martindale's dinner table a suitable place for…for such an inquisition. Excuse me.' She turned to her neighbour on the other side, who happened to be free, and began a conversation with him.

She had at least stopped laughing at him, he thought, with a certain amount of satisfaction. Really, what his aunt had said was perfectly right. Hester Perceval was an enigma, and would repay further observation. But not tonight—the girl was right, of course. His aunt's dinner table was not the place for serious investigation. And, to anyone who did not know how important it was to decipher the French papers as quickly as possible, his pursuit of Euclid must seem illogical, against the conventions of good society. But he would tackle Lowell Perceval very soon on his own ground and, meanwhile, he would watch Miss Perceval more closely.

Dungarran could observe without being observed when he chose to. And for the next week he observed Hester Perceval. He saw with surprise how animated her conversation with Lowell Perceval's young friends could be, what a teasing, laughing relationship existed among them all. He saw her dancing, obviously enjoying every minute, and displaying a marked grace. But not with anyone who could be classed as 'an eligible young man'. Her partners were members of her own family, friends of her parents, friends of her younger brother. As soon as she was asked to dance with anyone who had been in London six years before, or anyone who could be regarded as husband material, she stiffened and went silent and unresponsive. The transformation was amazing.

* * *

A few days later he was with his godmother being driven along Piccadilly when they saw Miss Perceval entering Hatchard's bookshop. 'Robert, look! Here's our chance. Biggs! Stop here! I wish to get down. Come, Robert. Let's find out a little more about our young lady. Is she buying Sir Walter Scott's latest offering? Or is Byron her choice? Or what?'

'She doesn't like poetry,' said her godson grimly, as they entered the shop, 'but I can see one thing— Miss Perceval is once again walking out with neither groom nor maid to accompany her. And in Piccadilly, too!'

'Shocking. But never mind that. I want to see what she does. Come!' They saw Miss Perceval had walked past the tables displaying novels and poetry, and was standing in front of a shelf holding a variety of scientific works. Even as they entered she started talking earnestly to an assistant there.

Dungarran put his hand on his aunt's arm. 'Don't go any further!' he said quietly. Picking up a fine volume of *Ackermann's Views of London* from a table by the door, he added, 'We'll look at this for a moment or two.' After a while Hester Perceval turned and made her way back towards the entrance. She was carrying a small parcel. He intercepted her.

'Why, Miss Perceval!' he said. 'What a surprise to find you here!'

'Lord Dungarran! Lady Martindale! How…how pleasant to see you.' She didn't look as if she was pleased. In fact, she had turned a little paler. But she rallied and said, 'What a splendid shop this is! I could spend hours looking at it all.'

'You appear to have bought something.'

She looked at the parcel in her hand as if she had forgotten it. 'This? Oh, yes! P...poems.'

'I thought you didn't like poetry?'

She looked blank for a moment. 'Oh yes! No! I mean, since coming to London I have decided that I should find out more about it, Lord Dungarran.'

'A great deal of nonsense is talked about poetry, Miss Perceval,' said Lady Martindale, smiling. 'There are some excellent poets, of course—but some very bad ones, as well. I find Lord Byron's effusions quite ridiculously overvalued. Do you?'

'I... I haven't read any. Yet. Whom do you admire, Lady Martindale?'

They talked for some minutes, at the end of which Dungarran said, 'My aunt's carriage is outside. May we offer you a lift back to Bruton Street, Miss Perceval? Or would you prefer to walk?'

'Thank you, but I would prefer to walk. The...the exercise is good for me.'

He looked at her sardonically. 'Then I'll call your footman, shall I? Or is your maid with you?'

Lady Martindale took pity on Miss Perceval's dilemma. 'I have a better idea, Robert. I should like to take Miss Perceval back to Grosvenor Street with me. I should like to show her the picture of her grandmother painted by one of my aunts when they were both young. A watercolour. Hugo says he can still trace a likeness, even after all these years. I would dearly like you to see it, too, Miss Perceval. Can you spare the time?'

Hester hesitated. She was strongly tempted. Lady Martindale had a most attractive manner.

'Do come,' said Lady Martindale persuasively. 'Robert can walk back. We'll look at the picture and chat until he arrives, and then we shall all have tea together. Would that not be charming?'

Robert Dungarran saw with amusement that, like many another before her, Hester was slightly dazed, but unable to refuse Lady Martindale. His aunt had a way of making it impossible. He handed the ladies into the carriage and watched them drive off. Then he went back into the shop. The assistant, who knew him well, was very ready to oblige.

'The young lady has made several purchases in the last week or two, my lord. But I'm afraid I was unable to oblige her today in her chief request. She wished to purchase, on her brother's behalf, I understand, something on the recent researches into calculus. I suggested he might more likely find such a work in Cambridge. The subject is somewhat remote for our London clientele.'

'Were you able to help her with anything else, Behring?'

'Yes! We had a volume of Mr Lagrange's dissertations on number theory and algebraic equations, which she bought. In French, naturally. But she assures me that her brother is fluent in French.'

'An erudite young man.'

'Oh, very. If I remember correctly, you have such a volume yourself, my lord.'

'I believe I have. Thank you, Behring.'

Dungarran walked along Piccadilly and through Berkeley Square towards Grosvenor Street so deep in thought that he completely ignored the greetings of several passers-by. Such discourtesy was so unlike him that his friends were quite worried. They would have been even more concerned if they had seen his behaviour a few minutes later. On the far side of Berkeley Square he stopped abruptly, paused, then turned round and strode swiftly back to his own house in Curzon Street. He reappeared a few minutes later carrying a small parcel and resumed his progress to his aunt's house.

Here he found his aunt and Hester Perceval in animated conversation over the teacups. A watercolour of a young lady lay on the table.

'Where have you been, Robert? As you see, we found we couldn't wait any longer—we have started without you.'

Dungarran helped himself to tea, and settled himself comfortably in a chair opposite his aunt's visitor. He had already placed his parcel on a small table beside the chair.

'What do you have there, my dear?' asked Lady Martindale. 'It looks like a book. From Hatchard's? Did you return there? Is that what kept you?'

'Which question would you like me to answer first, Godmama? Yes, it is a book. Yes, I did go back into

Hatchard's. No, the book is not from there. It is one of my own, which I propose to lend to Miss Perceval. I understand she would be interested in it.'

Hester shifted uneasily under Dungarran's steady gaze. His last words had surprised her, and she made an effort to smile gratefully. 'Thank you, but if it is poetry, Lord Dungarran, I cannot promise to read it with great understanding—more as a willing beginner.'

'That may well fit the case exactly, Miss Perceval, though I'm afraid it isn't poetry.' With these words he got up and handed the parcel to Hester. She hesitated. He seemed to tower over her, and there was something in his manner which was not reassuring. She threw a look of appeal at Lady Martindale, who said, 'Pray open it, Miss Perceval! I am most intrigued. I cannot imagine what it is. Do tell me.'

Reluctantly Hester undid the string and unwrapped the book. She looked at it in silence for a moment while she felt a wave of scarlet colour her cheeks.

'It…it is a book on calculus,' she said in strangled tones.

'I understand from Behring that you were asking about such a work.' Then he added sardonically, 'For your brother, of course.'

Lady Martindale, looking concerned, came over and sat by Hester. 'Robert, I am not certain I approve—'

'Please, Aunt Martindale. I surely do not have to remind you, of all people, how urgent the matter is.'

Hester had not heard this exchange. After the initial

shock she concentrated on rallying her forces. This detestable man with his spying ways had nearly reached the end of his search for Euclid. But she was not about to give in without a fight.

She stood up and said coldly, 'Am I to understand, Lord Dungarran, that you questioned a tradesman about my activities? A shop assistant? You must allow me to tell you that even in Northamptonshire we would not consider that to be the action of a gentleman!'

'You are right, of course, and I apologise—I am only sorry that it was necessary.'

'Necessary! To whom? To you? To satisfy your own idle curiosity?' The scorn in Hester's voice was devastating.

Lady Martindale, who had been prepared to intervene on Miss Perceval's behalf, sat back and decided to wait. Life in London was often rather dull, but this tea party promised to be much more interesting than the usual insipid exchange of gossip. It looked as if the unmasking of Euclid was imminent—which in itself was exciting. Meanwhile, she would enjoy watching Hester Perceval attempting to hold her own, even against her masterful nephew—and, all things considered, she was doing rather well, too.

'But then I should have learned,' Hester continued with equal contempt. 'Necessity has a habit of causing you to forget you were born a gentleman! Prying into my affairs today is no worse than hitting me, defenceless as I was, six years ago. You claimed necessity then, if I remember.'

'Robert! You didn't!'

Dungarran smiled grimly at his aunt's startled protest. 'It is, sadly enough, perfectly true, Godmama. I ought to tell you in my own defence that Miss Perceval was in the grip of raging hysteria at the time. Nothing else would have got through to her.'

Lady Martindale looked quite fascinated. 'I never realised that your earlier acquaintance with Miss Perceval was so…eventful,' she said.

Dungarran ignored his aunt's curious gaze. He turned to Hester and smiled disarmingly. 'But I assure you, I have regretted that, and what I said afterwards, ever since. Can you forgive me?'

Hester was not to be placated. 'Fine words! But your 'regret' does not seem to have inhibited your ungentlemanly conduct today!'

With delight Lady Martindale noted that her nephew, unaccustomed as he was to having his charm ignored, was disconcerted. He said sharply, 'If we are talking of ungentlemanly conduct, ma'am, may I remind you of your own present behaviour?'

'What do you mean? I don't know what you mean! Explain yourself, sir!'

'I should have thought my meaning was obvious to the poorest intelligence—and we both now know that yours is far from that, my dear Miss Perceval. Since coming to London you and your scapegrace of a brother have done your best to deceive me. Evasions, half-truths, lies, even—'

'We did not lie!'

'Oh? I suppose you really do have one or two

books of poetry in your possession? The first one was ballads, was it not? Lent to you by brother Lowell?'

Hester turned away suddenly. 'The first one,' she said in a low voice. 'The first one… It…it wasn't mathematics, I promise you.'

'And the rest?'

When Hester remained silent he said, 'It would not have been necessary to question servants and shop assistants if you had been more forthcoming with the truth.'

Hester recovered her voice. 'But why on earth should we? What is it to you?'

'We shall come to that later. Meanwhile, Miss Perceval, will you finally admit that you were Lowell's companion at that lecture? I should tell you that there can be no other explanation.'

Hester glanced at Lady Martindale, then sighed. 'Yes. Yes, I was. Is it not shocking? Dressing up as a man, and braving a masculine preserve? Does that satisfy you? You can surely condemn my behaviour now, Lord Dungarran.'

'On the contrary—if it was the only way you could hear such an excellent lecture then I admire you for your enterprise. I expect your brother had a hand in it, too. But this is unimportant—'

'Unimportant? Do you realise what it would mean if society got to know of it? I should have to retire once again in disgrace. My parents would be devastated.'

'There is no reason at all why the world should hear anything at all of the matter. I have far more important things on my mind than tattling to society, and my aunt's discretion is world-famous. But tell me—does this mean that you are prepared to admit that you are indeed Euclid?'

Hester paused. Her mind was racing, but she was forced to discard one evasive explanation after another. Dungarran would never now believe that either Hugo or Lowell could cope with the work she had been doing. There was no one else. Finally, she said simply, 'Yes.'

Lady Martindale got up and kissed her. 'Brave girl! Wonderful girl!'

Dungarran was shaking his head. 'Incredible girl! What a dance you have led me! My aunt was the first to suggest it, but I refused to believe her.' He gazed at her bemused. Then, still shaking his head in amazement, he said, 'My dear Miss Perceval, let me tell you at once what a delight my correspondence with Euclid has been.'

'I… I cannot tell you how much I have gained from my association with Zeno,' Hester said shyly.

'Give me your hand.' Hester slowly raised her hand and Dungarran took it in his own and kissed it. Hester looked at his bent head. This man holding her in his own strong, warm hands, his lips on her fingers, was Zeno, her friend, her mentor, her inspiration… She had never imagined anything like this… A feeling of purest delight, unlike anything she had ever experienced before, ran through her veins like fire. It frightened her and she snatched her hand from him and turned away, trembling. After a moment she added, 'I shall miss our work together.'

Chapter Seven

'Miss it? What do you mean?'

'I shall have to give it up. You must see that I cannot continue, not now that we both know the truth.'

Disappointment made Dungarran's tone sharp. 'Why the devil not?'

'Isn't it obvious? Zeno was a friend—but you...? Oh no!'

'This is nonsense! I know you dislike me—you have made that very clear. But you can surely forget Robert Dungarran. I'm still Zeno!' He took her firmly by the shoulders and turned her back to face him. 'And I need you more than ever! You must not give up! I won't let you!'

Hester shook herself free. 'Who do you think you are—to tell me what I must do or not do! You cannot force me to work with you! Indeed, I would find it impossible! I am astonished, Lord Dungarran, that you still wish to do so, now that you know Euclid is such an ill-educated, ignorant, conceited fool of a girl!'

'Damn it, why do you have to throw in my face words uttered six years ago in the direst circumstances. I've told you I regret saying them—though they were true enough at the time—'

'Ha! And I suppose you haven't considered me stupid and dull since?'

'Well, yes— But that was before—'

Lady Martindale, who had been sitting forgotten, decided it was time to intervene.

'Children, children,' she said. 'This discussion is clearly going nowhere. Sit down, Miss Perceval. Robert has something to explain to you. It is important. Please, sit down.'

Hester, looking mulish, sat down again on the sofa. Dungarran, with a nod of thanks at his aunt, took a deep breath and began to explain the situation he faced in the matter of deciphering the French papers.

He spoke well and clearly, but Hester was hardly listening. Six years of regaining confidence, of learning to be tolerant, of developing a sense of humour, had vanished like the wind. She was filled with the old fury against the young men who had so humiliated her six years before, chief among them this man. Stupid and dull, indeed—that's what he thought her! It did not occur to her that, since returning to London, she had done her best to convince society in general, and Dungarran in particular, that she was both. She quite forgot that she had enjoyed deceiving him, persuading him that she was the ninny he thought her.

The logic and balance so superbly evident in Euclid's work were notably absent for the moment—swamped under Hester Perceval's purely feminine sense of insult. No! It was impossible to think of Zeno as separate from Robert Dungarran. She would not even try. When he had finished she shook her head and stood up.

'I am sorry. The trust and confidence I had in Zeno have gone—I only see Lord Dungarran. I do not think I would be *able* to work with you. Besides, what would society say about the amount of time we should have to spend in each other's company? How could I explain that? No, I am honoured, of course, Lord Dungarran, but there must be others—'

'Dammit, there is no one else! Why the devil do you think I've spent so much time and energy seeking you out? Oh, ye gods! Why did Euclid have to turn out to be a woman?'

Hester turned triumphantly to Lady Martindale. 'You see, ma'am? It is exactly as I have always said. Men are incapable, completely incapable, of doing justice to a woman's intelligence! Now that your nephew knows Euclid is female, look how his attitude has changed! If I were idiotic enough to agree to work with him my efforts would soon be dismissed as irrational and foolish, and he would, in no time at all, cease to have any confidence in what I did. And he expects—no! He *demands* that I should help him! Ha!'

Lady Martindale said gently, 'You are doing my nephew an injustice, Miss Perceval. But I think that neither of you is in a state at the moment to discuss this very important subject sensibly and without prejudice. May I suggest that he calls on you tomorrow morning, when you have both had time to reflect?' She turned to her nephew. 'Meanwhile, Robert, I should like you to escort Miss Perceval back to Bruton Street,' adding with a smile, 'but may I advise you not to mention Zeno, or Euclid, or ciphers on the way? Talk about the weather, or the latest fashions— or even poetry!' She took Hester's hand. 'My dear, I congratulate you. Whatever Robert may have said, no one's work in ciphers has impressed him more than yours. Remember that when you are considering what to do. I shall see you very soon, I hope.'

The walk back to Bruton Street was accomplished almost in silence. Hester's thoughts were in turmoil, and her companion seemed preoccupied. At her door he bowed and handed her the two books which had precipitated the scenes at Lady Martindale's.

'At what time may I call tomorrow?' he said calmly.

'I keep early hours—country hours, you might say. I am usually available from ten o'clock. But it will do you no good—'

'Please! We promised my aunt we would not discuss the matter today.' He pointed to the book on calculus. 'Start reading this one. You will be fascinated, I assure you.'

She looked at him suspiciously, but he was completely serious. 'Thank you,' she said. He took her hand, and kissed it. The gesture was a conventional one—not at all like the kiss he had pressed on her fingers at Lady Martindale's. But even so, she experienced a faint echo of the same tingling sensation. This would not do! She moved somewhat jerkily away, bowed her head briefly and, avoiding his eyes, went in.

'Hester! Hester! Was that Lord Dungarran with you?' Her mother's voice greeted her as she entered the salon. 'Where have you been, child? I've been expecting you this age.'

'Lady Martindale invited me to tea, Mama, and Lord Dungarran kindly escorted me home.' Hester was unable to suppress an ironic smile at this tame description of a somewhat fraught afternoon. Her mother, seeing the smile, drew her own conclusions.

'How kind! I have always admired Dungarran. He has such style—and such an eligible young man, too!'

'Mama, believe me, for I mean it very sincerely, I will not change my mind about men and marriage— least of all in favour of Lord Dungarran. Indeed, if anything, I have become more than ever convinced that I would prefer to remain a spinster. Can we not return to Northamptonshire quite soon? Surely I have satisfied your conditions?'

'But Hester! It is far too soon to leave London! Why, we are only in the second week of June.'

'But Robina has left London, and the Cleeves as well. Can't we go too?'

'Be patient, Hester. We shall stay a little longer. Your father and I are enjoying London life, and it is so delightful to see Hugo again.'

Hester gave up. She was not to escape further acquaintance with Dungarran, it seemed. What her mother would say when he called the very next morning she could not begin to think!

The Bruton Street house had a small room to the right of the entrance, where the occupant of the house could entertain casual visitors. The next morning Hester waited there for Dungarran. She had not changed her mind overnight, but she was by no means clear quite why. His plea for help was a reasonable one, though she could hardly believe that her expertise was so vital to the country. But in some indefinable way she felt that this man was a threat to her peace of mind, her settled way of life, and she wanted no more to do with him. The curious feeling his touch had roused in her had not been unpleasant—far from it—but it represented danger, she was sure. So she faced him with determination.

'I expect to return to Northamptonshire quite… quite soon,' she said. 'Communication would be too difficult.'

'I agree the distance would complicate matters, but we've managed well enough for several years—why is it suddenly impossible?'

'Lowell was my messenger, and he does not plan to come to Abbot Quincey so frequently in the future.'

'I can have packages sent—'

'No! That…that would not do.'

'For God's sake let us quit these prevarications.

Miss Perceval, I don't think you understand how important these documents are—'

'I don't care how important you may believe the documents to be! I am not going to help you! Do you understand?'

'Oh yes, I understand. I understand very well. You will let your dislike of me override everything else— your love of the work, your sense of duty, your patriotism...all must give way to Miss Perceval's grudge—which she has cherished for six long years— against this monster Dungarran, who, God knows, doesn't deserve it. Can you be surprised that I despise the pettiness of such a mind? That my opinion of Euclid is seriously affected by what I hear from you?'

The door suddenly opened and Lowell burst into the room. He did not observe Dungarran, who was standing behind the door.

'I say, Hester! Have you heard? No, you can't have done, it won't be in the papers till tomorrow. Sywell has been murdered! And it's just as you described Rapeall's end in your book—every detail! The razor, the blood all over the bedchamber, Sywell was even in his nightshirt... The resemblances are uncanny! By Jupiter, this ought to increase the sales of *The Wicked Marquis* no end!'

Hester had been trying in vain to stem Lowell's flow. But now he saw her gestures, turned and saw the figure by the door.

'Oh my Lord!' he said.

'Exactly,' said Dungarran grimly. He surveyed them. Finally he said, 'You are full of surprises, Miss

Perceval, some more pleasant than others. Do I gather from this that you are the author of *The Wicked Marquis*?'

Lowell would have said something but Hester silenced him with a gesture. 'Yes,' she said. 'Have you read it?'

'I have—as have all your other victims. You have a gift for satire. The pictures you drew of us all were cruel, but very funny. I take it they were based on your experiences in London six years ago?' Hester nodded, and he went on, 'But the rest—the cheap sensationalism, the salacious details… Were they perhaps based on experience, too?' He stopped and stared at her. For a moment there was in his gaze a boldness, a contemptuous familiarity which Hester had never in her life seen directed towards her by anyone.

'How dare you, sir!' she exclaimed. She lifted her chin and stared back angrily, but she could not sustain it. After the briefest of moments the full significance of what he had said overcame her and her eyes dropped. Her hands moved in a gesture of repudiation, as she turned away, her head bent in shame.

Lowell took a step forward. 'Sir, I—'

Dungarran turned to Lowell. He said softly, but so dangerously, 'Ah yes! I should have known! It was you! By heaven, it was you! Her brother! She could never have written those descriptions, not in a lifetime. You did!' When Lowell nodded miserably, Dungarran exploded. 'By God, you may have done some reckless things in your time, Lowell Perceval, but you have never done a more wicked one! And you claim to love your sister! What the hell do you mean by exposing her to the sort of comment that book aroused? Putting her in danger of the censure of most of society, and the lewd curiosity of the rest! If she were ever discovered she would most certainly be an outcast for the rest of her days—even her parents might well disown her. You are despicable!' He went over to Hester, who was standing with her back to them, battling against the tears which threatened to overcome her. His voice softened. 'Miss Perceval, forgive me, please forgive my over-hasty words of a moment ago. Believe me, I was so shocked I hardly knew what I was saying. I swear I did not mean them.'

Hester swallowed. 'I... It was understandable, I suppose. As soon as I saw what Lowell had written I knew I should not have allowed it.'

'By heaven, you should not! Were you mad? How could you let your partiality for this half-witted scoundrel blind you to the risks you were taking?'

Hester swallowed. 'I... I—'

'I stole the book,' said Lowell sulkily. 'I took it from her cupboard. She never intended to have it published. I added the saucy bits. She didn't know anything about it before she came to London, and by that time it had been on the town for weeks.'

Hester wiped her cheeks and said firmly, 'But the original idea was mine. If I had not written the book in the first place Lowell would never have been tempted. So what…what do you propose to do, Lord Dungarran?'

'What do you think I should do? Your brother has put you in danger of complete ostracism from decent society. Do you not think that he deserves some sort of punishment?'

'I'll take whatever you can devise, sir, if you could spare my sister from public disgrace.'

'You should have thought of the public disgrace before you embarked on this latest lunatic escapade!' Dungarran said in biting tones. He paused in thought while the two Percevals regarded him in silence. Finally he said slowly, 'Your parents are the proper people to deal with this, but I am reluctant to give Sir James such a shock. Perceval, I would like to talk to your sister in private. Perhaps you could leave us alone for a few minutes?'

Lowell looked doubtfully at Hester, but she nodded. 'Don't worry, Lowell. Things will be all right, you'll see.' Uncertain and ashamed he went out, closing the door softly behind him.

'Have you always spoilt him, Miss Perceval? Saved him from his just deserts?'

'Not at all. Lowell has been a great help to me in the past, especially after I returned from London six years ago. It was he who introduced me to the New Scientific and Philosophical Society, which led to the…the work on ciphers. I think that saved my sanity. You and your friends had almost destroyed me. His efforts then did much to repair the damage. Oh no, I owe Lowell more than I could ever repay.'

'He has something to his credit, then. But all the same, he should not escape punishment for this piece of madness. Do you realise the potential seriousness of what he has done to you? My reaction was mild compared with what you might meet with from others.'

'I…do now. And I am sure he is aware of it, too.'

'Perhaps I should consult Hugo…'

'No! Not Hugo!' Hester cried. Dungarran looked at her in amazement. She went on, 'Please, you don't understand. I am sure that Hugo is a very good friend. And he is the best of brothers, too. But his standards are impossibly high for someone as…as volatile as Lowell. I cannot imagine that any good would come of involving Hugo.' She stopped. It went sorely against the grain to plead with this man, but she bit her lip and said stiffly, 'Could you not simply forget that you ever heard Lowell's words this morning? I would do anything to save him from the loss of Hugo's good opinion.'

Dungarran considered her in silence. Then he smiled, that dangerous, charming smile, the sort to charm an unwary bird out of a tree. Hester just had time to think, 'But I am not an unwary bird, and I will not be charmed!' before he spoke.

'I should not allow your brother to escape, I know. But I will do it on one condition, Miss Perceval.'

'Which is?'

'That you remain in London, of course, and work with me on the French ciphers.'

'I knew it would be that!' Hester said bitterly. 'You are blackmailing me, sir.'

'Of course I am!'

'You have no gentlemanly scruples about it?' He shook his head with a little smile and she added with scorn, 'Naturally not. No doubt you will claim necessity!'

'I do. You may think of me as you will, but I will do anything to have these transcriptions done as soon as possible. Perhaps you should remember that I am doing you—and your family—a considerable favour in remaining silent about that book.'

Hester looked at him with dislike. Then she shrugged and asked, 'Where are we to work? It won't be easy to arrange without stirring up unwelcome gossip. Or do considerations of that sort not affect you?'

'I had thought that my aunt might help. Surprisingly, she has developed a liking for you.' The corner of his mouth twitched. 'Especially since you proved her right on Euclid's identity... You should get on very well with each other. You resemble her in so many ways. Like yourself, she has strong views on the manner in which women are treated in the world.'

Hester looked at him in astonishment. 'I have never heard her expound them!'

He raised an eyebrow. 'Perhaps she is...wiser in the ways of society than an inexperienced seventeen-year-old once was? I think you would be surprised at how much influence she has in certain important circles. But this is by the way—to business! My aunt is prepared to put a room in her house at our disposal. We could meet in the mornings, before half of London is awake. It means you would have to visit Lady Martindale rather more often than you have done. Would your parents object?'

'Oh, no! Especially as…' She smiled with some irony. 'Especially as you are Lady Martindale's nephew. You must know that you are regarded as eminently eligible by most mamas, including my mother.'

'I hardly—'

'But you need have no fears on that score, Lord Dungarran,' Hester went on. 'I have no intention of marrying anyone at all—least of all you.'

'Succinctly, if unkindly put. I am relieved, however, to hear it.'

Hester added loftily, 'My interest in mathematics is far greater than my interest in a possible partner.'

'Strange! That is exactly what my aunt says of me. We should make an ideal pair—that is to say, ideal colleagues. How soon can you arrange to visit my aunt? I can have the papers at Grosvenor Street to-morrow.'

'Then I shall come tomorrow. At ten?'

'Ten it is.' He came across and took her hand. To her relief he made no attempt to kiss it. 'Miss Perceval, I shall do my best not to irritate more than I can help. And, in spite of our differences, may I say how relieved I am to have Euclid as my co-worker?'

She looked at him coldly, not giving an inch. 'I hope I deserve your confidence. In return, I shall try not to let my dislike of being coerced into it interfere with my work for Zeno.'

He said softly, 'You have now given me your word that you will do this work with me. You cannot change your mind. The consequences, if not for yourself, then for Lowell, could be serious.'

The short, difficult silence was only broken when Lady Perceval erupted into the room.

'Hester! Why did you not tell me that Lord Dungarran was here? Please, sir, forgive my daughter's rag manners and allow me to offer you some refreshment. My husband is upstairs. I am sure he would be delighted to speak to you. And we expect Hugo any moment.'

Lord Dungarran allowed himself to be ushered out of the door and up the stairs to the salon. Hester followed demurely. It was plain that her earlier words to her mother were being ignored—Lady Perceval had not abandoned her hopes of a match. She was wasting her energies, but she only had herself to blame! As Hester went up the stairs she thought how strange it was that, however much she disliked Dungarran, she trusted him. She was quite confident that, having given his word, he would keep her secrets. Dislike him she might, but of his integrity she was certain.

In the salon Sir James was sitting by Lowell, looking very shocked. 'This is a shocking affair!'

'My dear, what are you talking about?' asked Lady Perceval. 'What has Lowell been telling you?'

'He says that that villain Sywell has been murdered!'

'Oh! Oh! Never say so!'

'Lowell seems to have it on good authority. Did
you ever know him, Dungarran?'

'No, Sir James. His adventures were before my
time, but if his recent reputation is anything to go
by… He's from your part of the country, is he not?
Doesn't he own Steepwood Abbey?'

'Yes, but it was never rightly his. Sywell won it
from its true owner eighteen or nineteen years ago.
That was a black day for all of us.'

'What happened?'

'It was back in '93. Edmund Cleeve was the Earl
then. He was told that his only son had died and
seemed to go mad. He came to London, came across
his old friend Sywell and they started gambling. But
Edmund Cleeve's luck was right out. In one night he
lost everything—Abbey, lands, wealth…everything.
They all went to Sywell.'

'Cleeve shot himself, didn't he?'

'Aye, that he did. And Sywell has lived in the
Abbey ever since. It's been a sorry business for the
neighbourhood. The land hasn't suffered too badly—
he sold a good deal of the estate back to Thomas
Cleeve. But it's not that. He's a man of no morals at
all, and his scandalously villainous behaviour has
brought misery and disgrace to many a poor girl in
the neighbourhood.' Sir James looked at his wife.
'But no more of that before the ladies.'

'I've heard the stories,' said Lord Dungarran

gravely. Hester threw him a quick glance, but he ignored her. 'I don't suppose there'll be many to mourn him.'

'Least of all Thomas Cleeve. After he inherited the title he badly wanted to buy back the Abbey itself, but Sywell would never sell. For years Thomas has had to watch the ancestral home of the Earls of Yardley falling into ruin without being able to do a thing about it. I wonder if he knows about the murder?'

'I doubt it,' said Lowell. 'It's not yet generally known.'

'And the Cleeves have left London,' added Lady Perceval. 'My dear, these are unpleasant topics of conversation. I didn't invite Lord Dungarran up here for this!'

Sir James seemed not to have heard her. He frowned. 'It means there'll be some changes round the district.'

'For the better, I would think. But... I really came this morning with a request from Lady Martindale. She was most interested in the work Miss Perceval has been doing, and I've come with a request for a further opportunity to talk to her. Is that possible?'

Lady Perceval was clearly delighted. Apart from her relationship to Dungarran, Lady Martindale was one of society's most influential hostesses. 'Of course!' she cried. 'What work is this, Hester?'

'Er...something I was working on in my attic, Mama. You remember I was studying Grandpa Perceval's papers? It's something arising from that which interested Lady Martindale.' Hester smiled affectionately at her mother. 'So you see, Mama, that not everyone thinks books a waste of time for a woman! I could work with her in the mornings. I would still be free for…for visits and social occasions.'

'Well, if Lady Martindale wishes…'

'Thank you!' said Dungarran briskly. 'I'll call for you tomorrow morning, then, Miss Perceval. And now, alas, I'm afraid I must go. My aunt will be delighted that you have given your consent, Lady Perceval. Sir James, I hope this news of Sywell's death does not disturb your enjoyment of London. The world would seem to be well rid of such a scoundrel. Lowell—' He paused. 'Are you walking my way? I thought I would visit Tattersall's.'

Lowell looked a little apprehensive but agreed. The two men left together.

'My dear girl, what an opportunity! Lady Martindale moves in the very highest circles. Sir James, do you not think it wonderful?'

'Of course, of course.' Sir James seemed rather abstracted. The news of Sywell's death was clearly causing him some thought.

Hester sat without speaking. The morning's events had left her mind in turmoil. She was full of apprehension about working with Dungarran, though she knew she must. It would be foolhardy to arouse his displeasure. If she was reckless enough to go back on her word, not only would he take his revenge, but the delight and interest she had found for so long in the world of ciphers would be lost to her. The correspondence with the *Journal* would naturally cease.

But there were more positive arguments in favour of doing as Dungarran wished. She had found Lady Martindale an interesting and likeable woman, the first lady of fashion she had met who also cultivated the mind. The prospect of getting to know her better was an attractive one. And, she had to admit, now that she had been forced to cooperate with Dungarran she was growing interested in the work he had described—she knew she could do it.

True to his word, Dungarran called for her the next morning some minutes before ten o'clock. Hester was waiting, and they set off at a brisk pace. Apart from a few errand boys and tradesmen they saw no one on the way. London was still asleep. With any other companion Hester would have enjoyed the unaccustomed exercise. Walking was a favourite occupation at home in Abbot Quincey, and the rather tame promenades in the park, which was all she was offered in London, were no substitute.

'Lord Dungarran, it is kind of you to have fetched me this morning, but I would prefer to make my own way to Grosvenor Street in future,' she said as they drew close to their destination.

'I'm afraid that is simply not possible, Miss Perceval. This is not Northamptonshire. The streets of London are no place for an unaccompanied female.'

'I could use one of the footmen—'

'And how long would it be before you were dispensing with his services? No, I shall fetch you my-self. It is simpler and safer.'

'Oh, why do you always have to be so...so high-handed? Always to know better? You are as bad as Hugo!'

He turned and grinned at her—not the dangerously charming smile, but in genuine amusement. 'Such outrageous flattery is embarrassing. I have the highest possible regard for your elder brother! But you forget, Miss Perceval. I know you a good deal better than I did a month ago. You are, I have discovered, neither dull nor simple. Nor are you very biddable. Is the pot calling the kettle black?'

This made her laugh in spite of herself. When Lady Martindale received them she was pleased to observe that they were in a better humour with each other than she had seen before.

After leaving their coats with a servant they were shown into a light, airy room with two windows. Under each was a table with plenty of paper, ink, pens, a slate and chalk practically covering the surface. A comfortable chair was placed at each table in such a way that the sitters would have their backs to each other.

'I thought it safer,' said Lady Martindale with a smile. 'But you seem to have settled some of your differences? I am so glad, my dear, that Robert has managed to persuade you to work on the ciphers.'

'His arguments were...very convincing, Lady Martindale. I found myself unable to refuse.'

Robert Dungarran cast a glance at Hester. Her blue

eyes were innocent of guile, her voice conventionally polite. His aunt was unconscious of any double meaning. The delicate irony of her words was meant solely for him, he was sure. How could he have missed till now the wit and subtlety of this girl? How many times must he have overlooked the hidden humour, the barbs behind her façade of demure nonentity! How often had she made a fool of him without his even noticing? Well, those days were over. He had Miss Perceval's measure, and they were now battling on equal terms. He said easily, 'Don't count on the peace lasting, Godmama. I am still a monster in Miss Perceval's eyes. But we mustn't waste time. Where are the papers?'

'I locked them in the bureau here.' Lady Martindale went to a substantial but beautiful bureau in the corner of the room, and opened the front. She took out an untidy bundle of papers and handed them to her nephew, who spread them out on one of the tables.

'The ones I've already transcribed are on top,' he said to Hester. 'I thought they would be useful for comparison. Do you remember the St Cloud set?'

'St Cloud? I don't think I ever saw...'

'Ah yes! You did, but we didn't tell you what they actually were. Do you remember a rigmarole about Caesar and Gaul and crossing the Alps?'

'Ah, those! Yes. I thought they were nonsense, but they were a real challenge to solve.'

'There are more like them,' he said grimly. 'It's a slow business deciphering them.'

Hester hardly heard him. She was already sitting down at the table, eagerly perusing one of the papers. After a moment she took a pen and started jotting down a set of numbers. Lady Martindale smiled, took out a book, and made herself comfortable in an armchair by the bureau. Lord Dungarran looked at Hester, shook his head in a bemused fashion, then sat down at the other table with another of the documents. The silence was complete except for the occasional scratching of a pen.

Chapter Eight

When Hester got up to go at the end of that first morning, she was disconcerted to find both Lady Martindale and her nephew regarding her with amusement. Somewhat stiffly she asked if there was something wrong with her appearance.

'You look delightful, my dear!' said Lady Martindale. 'But unless you wish to have your activities questioned on this very first day, you had better remove a telltale spot of ink from the end of your nose!'

'Is there one? Oh, it's too bad! It always happens at home, but I tried so hard not to let it happen here!' Hester took out her handkerchief and scrubbed at her nose.

'Not that side—allow me,' said Dungarran, smiling broadly. He took her handkerchief, adjured her to lick it, then carefully wiped the offending stain. 'There!' he said. 'All gone. But I'm afraid there's some on your dress, too.'

Hester gave a cry of horror and looked down. A

spot of ink marred the bodice of her simple muslin gown. 'I don't know why it should be so,' she exclaimed. 'I take such pains, but there's always something!'

'I think that you forget to take such pains when you're working, Miss Perceval. I have seldom seen such complete concentration—especially not in a wo—'

'Be careful, sir!' Hester said in warning tones.

'In anyone,' he amended. 'But what will you do?'

'My maid will wash the muslin if I can just get to my room without seeing my mother. At home I use a large apron to cover me, but I didn't bring it to London.' She looked at him severely. 'I never suspected that I should need it!'

'I think I can help there, Miss Perceval,' said Lady Martindale hastily. 'I can find something for you. It will be here tomorrow. I should hate our little scheme to founder for want of an apron!'

The next morning she produced an ideal garment. It was very like the apron Hester used at home, of coarse material with a front bib, shoulder straps and a tie at the back. The chief difference was that it was in a bright, clear blue, not the dull grey that Hester was used to. Hester eyed it doubtfully.

'Put it on, Miss Perceval. It is not an elegant garment, but it will protect your dress. And the colour will suit you perfectly.'

The colour seemed to Hester to be far too vivid, but she shrugged and put it on. Then she thanked her hostess and sat down to work, losing herself almost immediately once more. Lady Martindale exchanged a smile with her nephew and sat down in her armchair by the bureau.

From then on Dungarran and Hester worked together in the room at Grosvenor Street. Lady Martindale read or sewed in her corner, occasionally looking up as one or other of them exclaimed or sighed, or took a paper over to the other table and consulted. There was nothing in the least romantic about their conversations, but Lady Martindale was beginning to think that Hester Perceval would be the ideal wife for her nephew. Though neither was aware of it, their rapport was very strong. In spite of Hester's initial antagonism, each had an almost instinctive understanding of the other's mind, and the sum total of their joint work was far greater than either would have achieved alone. There was as yet no sign of any physical attraction—but, Lady Martindale smiled to herself, that might come with time and propinquity!

Hester soon found that the mind of the unknown French ciphermaster was much in tune with her own. She had considerable success with a passage which had defeated the best minds at the War Office for months, and Dungarran's surprised, but perfectly genuine, admiration went a long way to make up for the humiliation of the past. She began to look eagerly for his approval, and in return was always ready to watch him use his own considerable, more intellectual, gifts to solve a problem which had defeated her. Though she was completely unaware of it, Hester's dislike of him was slowly but surely fading. Zeno, her friend and trusted guide, was imperceptibly becoming one with the figure of Robert Dungarran.

For his part he grew impatient with the tedious consultations at the War Office which kept him from her company. He wanted to be back with Hester Perceval in the room in Grosvenor Street, working with her to fathom the mysteries of the ciphermaster's mind. He rejoiced in the sight of the slender figure in blue, bending over her papers in such concentration. Even the spectacles which she had now taken to wearing for the work became an important part of the scene— and the usual spot of ink on her nose. Euclid, after all these years, had taken on a most surprising form!

The work went on apace, and the pile of papers was growing gratifyingly smaller when their plans received a sudden and unexpected threat.

The news of the Marquis of Sywell's demise had been dealt with in detail in the newspapers. 'It is with horror and dreadful dismay,' the *Morning Post* announced, the day after Lowell's revelations, 'that this paper has learned of the shocking death by stabbing of the most noble the Marquis of Sywell at his home, Steepwood Abbey, in the County of Northamptonshire earlier this week…' The paper, and others which took up the story, went on to describe in gory detail the scene which met the eyes of the Marquis's 'devoted retainer', Solomon Burneck, when he entered his master's bedroom on the fateful morning.

'"Devoted retainer", indeed!' muttered Sir James

rustling the paper impatiently. 'Partner in crime, more like! A more surly, unpleasant fellow I never met.'

'Did Burneck see the assailant? Or is he himself suspected?' asked Lady Perceval.

'The report gives no indication. As usual the press is short on facts and long on unnecessary and probably imaginary detail!' replied Sir James testily.

But if Sir James regarded the report as unsatisfactory, London did not. It was not long before the sparse details of the real-life death of the Marquis of Sywell were being compared with the fictional and far more sensational account of the murder of the 'Wicked Marquis'. The coincidences were very quickly remarked and in no time at all the details of the two murders were hopelessly confused. Rumour grew on rumour and soon the public imagination pictured the scene of the crime as a veritable blood bath, with indescribable atrocities inflicted on Sywell's corpse.

As a delicately bred female, Hester was spared the worst of the rumours. But in any case her preoccupation with the French documents left her little energy for the gossip and speculation which were flying round the capital.

Later in the week the newspapers, lacking any firm evidence or further facts, started to debate the consequences of the murder. This unsettled Sir James far more than any gruesome account of the crime.

'Lady Perceval! Listen to this!' he said, some days after the murder. He took up the newspaper and read out, '''The affairs of Lord Sywell are in some disar-

ray, and our correspondent tells us that inhabitants of
the surrounding villages, especially the tradesmen, are
already worried about unpaid bills and unsettled accounts. The future of the estate must be in doubt.
Following the mysterious disappearance of the
Marchioness last year, the Marquis lived alone, and
he appears to have no obvious heir. Moreover, surrounding landowners will also have their anxieties, as
long neglect has already led to disturbing occurrences
on the Steepwood estate.''' He got up and walked
restlessly round the room. His wife eyed him anxiously. After a while he said, 'It's a damnable affair!
As if the fellow had not caused enough trouble in his
lifetime! There's bound to be unrest in the district.
My dear, I must return to Northamptonshire as soon
as possible! Things will be in turmoil, and a good
many people will be looking to me to help them.'

'B… But Sir James! You must not leave London!'
exclaimed Lady Perceval. 'Just when Hester is at last
having some success! Lady Martindale has taken such
an interest in her this past week, and Lord Dungarran
has been really quite attentive. We cannot take her
away now!'

'What makes you think Robert attentive, Mama?'
asked Hugo, who was paying one of his frequent calls
on his parents. 'I have not seen any evidence of it—
and Hester seems to avoid him in public. Are you
sure you're not confusing the aunt with the nephew?
Lady Martindale certainly seems to have a strong liking for my sister, and I can see why—they are two
of a kind! But it would be unwise to resurrect Hester's

interest in Robert. Remember what happened last time!'

'I'm afraid I agree with Hugo, Lady Perceval! You set your hopes too high, my dear! I see no change whatever in Dungarran's attitude.'

'But given time…'

'You are always so optimistic! Why don't you listen to Hugo? He surely knows better.' Lady Perceval set her lips and remained obstinately silent. He sighed and added, 'Well, we shall no doubt eventually find out which of us is right…'

'But nothing will happen if Hester is removed from London just at this point, Sir James!'

'No. No, I quite see that.' He paused and thought for a minute. 'Would it suit if I went alone to Abbot Quincey and you and Hester stayed here?'

'Oh no! That would never do! I should be quite lost without you!'

He patted her hand. 'But what else can I do, my love?'

'Could I go, Father?'

Sir James regarded Hugo thoughtfully. 'It's certainly time for you to take a greater interest in the estate… But no. You couldn't do this alone. You've been in Abbot Quincey so seldom in the last few years that our people don't know you any more.'

Hugo said a little stiffly, 'I always promised to come back to Northamptonshire this year, Father. Before my thirtieth birthday.'

'Oh I don't blame you, my boy! I was very happy for you to enjoy town life before you settled down.

But you couldn't possibly deal with this situation. No, I must go myself.'

'Then I shall come, too! As you say, I ought to take up some of the responsibilities.'

Sir James beamed. 'Excellent! I shall be very pleased to have your support. It won't be an easy matter.'

'But what about Hester?' persisted Lady Perceval. 'If Hugo stayed in London she could remain with him!'

'My dear, you are talking nonsense! Hester couldn't possibly stay with Hugo in a bachelor's establishment! No, though I'm sorry for it, it looks as if you and Hester will have to come with us.' He took her hand and said persuasively, 'I should think she would be delighted to come back with us to Northamptonshire. Remember her reluctance to come here in the first place! Now, how soon can we be ready? Two days? One?'

Lady Perceval's pleas were in vain. Sir James remained adamant, and the family was informed that they would be returning to Northamptonshire very soon. But Sir James was wrong about Hester's reaction to the news. Such a short time ago, it was true, she would have given anything to leave London. But now the news dismayed her beyond measure. She was astonished at the depth of her disappointment.

When Dungarran heard of Sir James's plans he first of all swore comprehensively in private, then, in his usual calmly competent way, set about finding a way

out of the dilemma. After some thought he went back
to his aunt and asked for her help. She was equally
unhappy at the prospect of losing Hester Perceval's
company, but found what he proposed a little too un-
conventional.

'Invite Miss Perceval to be my house guest till the
end of the Season? I cannot do it, Robert!' she protested. 'I like Hester Perceval very much—I am sure
I would enjoy her company! But her parents will
surely think it extremely odd if a woman they hardly
know suddenly invites their only daughter to spend
several weeks with her, while the rest of her family
return to the country! And I trust you realise what
conclusion society would most certainly draw!'

'That I am interested in Miss Perceval? Well, I am,
though not in the way they might think!'

'That is all very well—but what of Miss Perceval?'

'Oh, you need have no scruples on that score,
Godmama. Hester Perceval has already declared in
the clearest terms that she has no interest in matri-
mony, least of all with me!'

'All the same, she will not enjoy the gossip which
is bound to arise.'

Her nephew was silent for a few minutes. Finally
he said, 'Well, perhaps we should encourage such
gossip. The idea that Miss Perceval and I are roman-
tically interested in each other would be an excellent
alibi for the time we already spend in each other's
company.'

'Really, Robert, I could get very angry with you!
You are so single-minded when it comes to your

work! What happens when the Season is over? Does Miss Perceval retire once again to Northamptonshire with a broken heart?'

'That is nonsense, you know it is! Yes, at seventeen she thought her heart was affected, but she soon grew up and recovered. She is now as clearsighted as I am about the sentimental rubbish talked of love.'

'But society will never believe it. And they will say that Miss Perceval has remained in London in the hope of capturing one of London's most eligible bachelors. You know how cruel people can be.'

'They won't say that, if we make it clear that I am the one in pursuit. Vain pursuit.'

'This is too complicated for me.'

Robert Dungarran took his aunt's hand. 'My dearest aunt, it will be very simple. I am positive that Miss Perceval is as eager as I am to complete this work. It only needs a week or two, but she must remain in London for that time. I shall pay Miss Perceval a great deal of attention in public, and she will carry on behaving towards me with her normal indifference verging on dislike. I think I could persuade her to act out our little comedy—especially if you were prepared to support us. There will be no danger to her reputation, I assure you!'

Lady Martindale smiled. 'If she is seen to reject the advances of London's eligible but elusive Lord Dungarran, her reputation can only be enhanced! You have been the target of every matchmaking mama for the past ten years!'

'Stop talking nonsense and tell me if you consent.'

'You must consult Hester first,' she said warningly.
'I will.'

'Then if the Percevals agree, I will help you. But I still think it is a madcap scheme!'

After Hester had most reluctantly agreed to Dungarran's plan, Lady Martindale approached the Percevals with her invitation. Persuasive though she was, it looked for a while as if their scheme would founder on Sir James's notions of what was proper, but she had an ally in Lady Perceval. Left alone with her husband, Hester's mother represented to him all the advantages of Lady Martindale's interest in their daughter.

'I am surprised, Sir James, that you even think of rejecting such a flattering invitation! I would not dream of arguing with your decision that we should return to Northamptonshire. I am sure your reasons are perfectly sound. But I hope I may claim some influence in a matter which so closely affects our daughter's prospects. You not only run the risk of offending one of society's great ladies, but you are also putting Hester's future at risk! I do hope you will reconsider.'

Hugo added his voice. 'Lady Martindale is just the sort of woman you would wish Hester to be, Father. She is undoubtedly as intelligent and as strong-minded as Hester, if not more so. I believe her to have quite an influence in government circles. But she has such tact, so much charm, that few people suspect this. Hester could learn a great deal from her.'

Sir James finally gave in to persuasion and Hester was allowed to accepted Lady Martindale's kind invitation. On the day the Percevals left London for Northamptonshire Hester was installed in a very pretty bedroom in the Grosvenor Street house. Lady Martindale made her most welcome, but spoke seriously to her before they came downstairs.

'Miss Perceval, I hope there are no unfortunate consequences to this scheme of Robert's. I wish you to promise that if you have any doubts about it—at any time—you will confide them to me. Though I am delighted to have your company, I am not at all sure that we are doing the right thing.'

'I hope you don't think the worse of me for agreeing?'

'Not at all. I consider you a brave woman.'

'Brave? In what way?'

'Robert can be very charming when he chooses—'

'Not to me, Lady Martindale. Pray have no anxiety on that score. I am in no danger from your nephew. I... I daresay you have heard what a fool I made of myself six years ago?'

'Something of it, yes. But it was a very long time ago. You were a mere child.'

'Perhaps. But the experience was enough to convince me that marriage was not for me.'

'I... I hope Robert was not the sole cause of such a harsh decision, Miss Perceval?'

'No. I don't even blame him—not now—for my disillusionment. I was a child and I misunderstood his intentions. I… I thought he was in love with me. But he was merely being a good friend to my brother.'

'My dear!'

'The shock caused me to…to behave very…very badly. It took six years to get over it.' Hester smiled wrily. 'I am most unlikely to make the same mistake again, I assure you.'

Lady Martindale looked at her closely and seemed satisfied with what she saw. She smiled brilliantly. 'Then let us enjoy ourselves with a clear conscience, Hester! Do say I may call you Hester!'

'I should like you to. But what do you mean "enjoy ourselves"? I am here to work.'

'My dear Hester, do but consider for a moment! You and Robert will of course continue to work as before—probably even harder. But in the evening we shall all be on public show. I am willing to wager that you will be more of a success than ever. But Robert? Will he enjoy playing the part of a rejected suitor? Such a role has so far been outside his experience! I wonder how he will cope?'

Hester smiled slowly at the picture conjured up by Lady Martindale's words. Then she said, 'Do you know, Lady Martindale, I think I am about to enjoy the social life of London for the first time in my life.'

Her hostess burst into laughter. 'Cruel, cruel girl!'

For a day or two there was a lull in London's festivities. Hester had a chance to settle into her new circumstances, including Robert Dungarran's constant presence. They worked harder than ever on the transcriptions, but the last few documents seemed to be more difficult than all the rest put together. The work which had been going so well suddenly came to a halt.

Halfway through one morning Hester threw her pen down, for once not minding that she spattered ink liberally over her apron front. 'I give up! I've tried everything I can think of. I thought I knew that Frenchman's mind, but this time he's been simply too clever for me! What the devil can he have used as a base?' She put her elbows on the table, rested her head on her hands, and gazed down in frustration at her scribbled efforts.

Dungarran leaned back in his chair with a sigh and stretched his long legs out before him. 'I haven't had any success, either! Damn the man! I've wasted half the morning on a single page.'

Lady Martindale looked at the two despondent backs. 'My dear children, you are both stale! You have been cooped up for far too long in this tiny room with nothing but the scratching of pens to entertain you! Give yourselves a rest from the puzzle and it may all become clear. Take Hester for a drive, Robert. It's time you were seen together in public.'

'As usual, you are right, Godmama. Come along, Euclid! Let's give our poor brains some fresh air. We'll have a drive round the park.' Hester got up without taking her eyes from her papers.

'Hester, dear,' said Lady Martindale patiently. 'Remove your apron, take off those hideous glasses and wipe your face, before you go. Otherwise the world will never believe our myth.'

'Myth?' asked Hester vaguely.

'The myth that I'm in love with you,' said Robert Dungarran, gently removing Hester's glasses. 'But I don't know that I agree with you, Godmama. There's something highly appealing about a suitably placed ink spot.' His finger touched Hester's nose. 'It draws attention to the purity of line…'

Hester, still abstracted, spoke much as she would have addressed Lowell. 'And I suppose you will say that this apron adds to my beauty?'

'It suits you.'

She looked up, startled. Then seeing his teasing smile, she pulled herself together. 'Thank you,' she said ironically. 'Well at least I know my place—a kitchenmaid! No, don't say another word—I shall clean myself up, then put on my hat and gloves. Though I doubt it will make an atom of difference to London's view of our relationship.'

When Hester had disappeared, Lady Martindale said, 'Did you mean it?'

'Mean what?'

'About the apron.'

'Well, I half meant it. I was teasing her. But yes, it does suit her.'

'It's the colour, of course. She always wears such insipid garments. As I said once before, her dresses are completely unmemorable, part of her desire to be invisible. But…if we are to convince society that she has attracted you…' Lady Martindale fell silent for a moment. Then she said suddenly, 'Robert, I will try to persuade Hester that she needs a new evening dress for the ball at Harmond House! You must help me.'

'How the devil do you think I could help? I can't imagine that Miss Perceval would be swayed by any recommendation of mine!'

'You must! But no more—here she comes! Hester! That's better. My dear, we've just been talking about the Duchess of Harmond's ball. It will be a splendid affair, and Robert has agreed to escort us both. It is a perfect opportunity to demonstrate his interest in you. How would it be if you had a new dress for the occasion?'

Hester said reluctantly, 'Mama insisted I needed one, but I already have so many...'

'This ball is worthy of another one,' said Lady Martindale firmly. 'And I know just the dressmaker you need—we shall pay her a visit this afternoon. I saw a bolt of absolutely lovely silk when I was last there—a dark azure blue peau-de-soie, just a shade deeper than the colour of your apron. It would be ideal.'

'Oh no! Thank you, but no! I always wear pale colours. Such a blue would be far too striking.'

'We could tone it down with an underdress of white, perhaps. Don't disappoint me, Hester dear. That blue suits you so well,' said Lady Martindale.

'So you have said, but I think not...'. Hester's tone demonstrated her reluctance to offend Lady Martindale, but it was quite firm.

'Robert, can't you add your persuasion?'

'I would…if I thought it necessary,' he drawled. 'Miss Perceval is right. She has somewhat in-sip…er…delicate colouring, and surely strong colours are better suited to…more dashing personalities?' Robert Dungarran noted with secret amusement that Hester's 'delicate colour' was rising in her cheeks. He went on, 'She is very wise to choose colours which suit her retiring nature. Besides which, unlike most of her sex, she is more interested in matters of the mind. Clothes which flatter, and the pursuit of beauty are beneath her. Fortunately.'

'Robert!'

'…Fortunately, I was about to say, for those of us who need her other skills.' He smiled charmingly at Hester, observing with pleasure that the colour was now high in her cheeks and that her fists were clenched inside her white gloves. He continued, 'But why are we wasting time on a topic which holds so little interest for Miss Perceval, Godmama? I'll wager that she believes clothes are meant to conceal our faults, not enhance our advantages.'

'I take it you mean the tailors' use of padding in the shoulders and stiffening in the jackets, sir?' Hester snapped, casting a glitteringly critical eye over Dungarran's excellent figure, his dark green coat immaculately smooth over broad shoulders and narrow hips. 'They certainly achieve marvels.'

Dungarran burst into laughter. 'Come, Miss Perceval! Enough sparring! We shall take some air. All this talk of dresses has wasted time which we can ill spare—especially if my aunt is taking you off to the dressmaker this afternoon. We still have to fathom the work of that ill-begotten son of a Frenchwoman.'

Nothing more was said, though Hester was noticeably silent on their drive. After their return Lady Martindale sought out her nephew in private and expressed strong disappointment in him.

'I cannot imagine what possessed you, Robert! You were unkind to Hester—and unfair! Her colouring is not at all insipid! And now she will insist on choosing yet another nondescript off-grey sort of colour, and the world will wonder what on earth you see in her! It's too bad of you!'

'Will you take a wager on the off-grey, dearest Godmama?'

Lady Martindale refused the wager, which was as well, for she would have lost it. On seeing the azure silk Hester said she had changed her mind, and declared it to be the very thing she was looking for. Madame Félice had received them graciously, for Lady Martindale had been one of her earliest patrons, but after a minute during which they discussed details of style, she apologised and asked if she might leave them in the competent hands of her assistant. She then withdrew. Hester was unmoved by this, but Lady Martindale was surprised, and said so.

'I expect she has large numbers of orders for the Harmond ball,' said Hester. 'And it's not as if I am likely to be a regular client. I really don't mind in the slightest. Compared with the seamstress at Abbot Quincey, any London dressmaker is a genius!'

It certainly seemed that Madame Félice's assistant was one. On the night of the ball Lady Martindale dressed early, and then sent Régine, her maid, along to Hester's room to add, she said, the final touches. Hester's own maid was young and inexperienced and very much in awe of Régine, who had come from France before the Revolution. She looked on while Régine dressed Hester's hair, and watched in admiration as the constricting bands of hair were undone, brushed vigorously, twisted and knotted by skilful fingers, and the whole finished off with a rope of pearls and crystal drops artfully arranged in the coils.

'But…but these are not mine. Where did they come from?' asked Hester.

'Her ladyship sent them, mademoiselle. And the earrings. Hold your head still, please, while I put them in… *Voilà!*'

Régine's tone was so businesslike that Hester felt she dared not argue. And when she looked at the result of the maid's ministrations she decided not to try. Her hair had been dressed by an expert, and for once it was evident that, along with her brothers, Hester too had inherited the famous golden gilt hair of the Percevals. Curling tendrils framed and softened the classical Perceval features, and behind them gleaming twists of hair dressed high emphasised the graceful line of head and neck. Pearls and crystals hung from delicate ears.

Régine allowed herself a small smile before she became businesslike again. 'Now for your dress.' Hester stood like a doll in her simple slip of white satin while the two maids twitched the heavy folds of deep blue silk into place. She was not used to such a low neckline, accustomed as she was to covering up her lack of curves with numerous frills of lace, and she twitched the bodice a little higher. Régine pursed her lips, pulled it back into place and said sternly, 'The neckline is perfectly modest, mademoiselle. You will spoil the line if you pull it so.'

'Of course,' said Hester meekly. 'It was just that I seem to have more…more figure than usual.'

'That is the art of cutting. I have not often seen such a beautiful piece of workmanship, no, not even in France. Would mademoiselle like to see herself?'

Hester stared at the figure in the looking-glass. Burnished hair glinting with stones, dark blue eyes wide with amazement, glittering drops at her ears, a slender throat, unmistakeable curves covered in satin overlaid with a simple layer of delicate white lace… All enhanced and enriched by the gleaming blue folds of silk.

Lady Martindale came in and clapped her hands. 'My dear girl!' she exclaimed. 'My dear Hester! Your hair! I never imagined… Régine, I congratulate you—that hair is divine!' Then she examined Hester from every side, and pronounced the dress a great success. 'The fit is excellent. Why have we never seen that very pretty figure before, Hester, my love?' Hester was still wondering what to reply when Lady Martindale smiled and said, 'But we must go down to the salon. Robert will be here shortly. I can't wait to see his face! Come, my dear.'

While they waited in the salon, Lady Martindale asked Hester if she had had a dress with a train before. 'They can be difficult to manage, but yours is a very small one. See? It has a tiny loop to hold it up when your are dancing. Yes, just like that! It really is a beautiful dress, Hester. A great success. Do you like it?'

'I... I'm not sure... I've never had anything as striking as this before.'

'You will be the belle of the ball, I swear. You must dance with Robert once, you know—he is our escort. But after that you can refuse him as often as you please.' Lady Martindale started laughing. 'London will be so sorry for him!'

'I can't wait to see it!' said Hester gleefully.

They were both still laughing when Dungarran was announced. If Hester had secretly hoped to see him struck dumb with admiration she was disappointed. He stopped, it was true, but merely to raise his eyeglass and examine her appearance with all his usual calm.

'Well, Robert? Admit you were wrong! That dark blue silk is perfect for Hester!'

'I knew it would be,' he said as he kissed his aunt.

'I beg your pardon?'

'I said I knew it would be.' He came over and smiled as he took Hester's hand to kiss. 'I also knew that Miss Perceval would be more likely to choose the blue if she believed I thought she should not. Am I right?'

'You...you...!' Hester controlled herself. She said

calmly, 'You are right, of course. How perceptive of you, sir. And how devious!'

'But in such a wonderful cause. May I say that you look magnificent, Miss Perceval? If I were a marrying man—'

'Which you are not.'

'I would find it impossible not to make reality of our myth tonight.'

'My dear sir,' said Hester, giving him a provocative look. 'If I were a marrying woman…'

'Yes?'

'I just might consider being more receptive. But as it is….' She smiled at him maliciously. 'Prepare to act the part of a rejected suitor, Lord Dungarran!'

Chapter Nine

Though a number of important families had already left London, enough were left behind to give lustre to the Duchess of Harmond's ball. As Dungarran entered the reception room accompanied by his two ladies, a perceptible stir ran round the room, and one or two eyeglasses were raised. Hester stiffened and her hand on Dungarran's arm tightened.

'Courage, my friend,' he said. 'Think of it as a play. I know you can act a part—I've seen you do it, and very cleverly, too! This can't be more difficult than acting the man!'

These words helped Hester through the following, nerve-racking minutes. So many of the ladies and gentlemen of the Ton, people who had in recent weeks practically ignored her, found some reason or other to talk to Lady Martindale and her protégée. While they made polite enquiries about her parents, they eyed her covertly, clearly wondering what had happened to dull, quiet Miss Perceval. In some cases their curiosity was so open that it verged on impertinence, and Hester could not prevent the colour from rising in her cheeks. But she remembered Dungarran's words and acted her part. After a few minutes it was no longer so difficult to be at ease with these people. The sense of failure, which had caused her to be stiff and awkward in society, had been replaced with the knowledge that in one sphere she was truly admired and valued for the work she had been doing. The man beside her, one of society's most influential members, was willing to let his unblemished reputation for success with the ladies suffer a severe setback rather than lose her. Hester lifted her head proudly and continued to astonish the Ton with her charm and self possession.

All the same, she was immensely relieved when Dungarran offered his arm and asked her to dance. And when he suggested taking a long way round via the conservatory she almost forgot to hide her approval of the idea.

They made their way through leafy pathways towards the huge ballroom at the back of the house.

'My congratulations. You're doing splendidly,' he said, looking down at her with a smile.

'I found it less difficult than I thought. And dancing is no longer the nightmare it once was.'

'You dance very gracefully, Miss Perceval.'

She felt the colour rising in her cheeks. 'We both know that I owe my skill to you in the first instance, sir,' she answered.

'But not much else,' he said abruptly. 'If you knew

how much I have regretted my cruelty to you all those years ago!'

She suddenly wanted to tell him how her attitude towards that disastrous début—and towards him—had changed. 'I can now see that I deserved something of what you said—perhaps not all. But I no longer brood on it, nor bear any grudges. During the past few years Zeno has done more than anyone to heal that injury. And only recently I've come to realise that in a curious way you and he have balanced it all out between you. So…shouldn't we forget the past? The present is so much more interesting! Don't you agree?'

'You look so enchanting that I would agree with anything at the moment, Miss Perceval! But this is not according to plan! You are supposed to be treating me coldly, not offering an armistice!'

'Well then, having said my piece, I will! Come sir! Enough of this tête-à-tête! I wish to dance!'

Hester had no shortage of dancing partners, though neither Lowell nor any of his friends was there to support her. Dungarran asked her to dance again and was refused, but he tried once more two-thirds of the way through the evening. Hester, who had found most of her partners tediously predictable in their remarks, was glad to accept, though she once again gave a show of reluctance. They took the floor for a set of country dances.

But halfway through a progression down the middle of the set Hester suddenly stopped. 'A pentacle!' she said. The couple behind cannoned into her, and a moment or two of confusion followed. Hester apologised gracefully, Dungarran shook his head with a deprecating smile at the rest of the set and they were soon under way again.

As soon as they were close enough he whispered, 'What happened?'

'It suddenly came to me. The base! It's not a rectangular grid—it's a pentacle! It could be, at least. It would account for the oddness in it.'

'You're talking of the cipher?'

She looked at him scornfully. 'Of course I am!'

'We'll try it tomorrow! That look of contempt was very convincing, by the way. I am suitably crushed.' They were separated again by the movement of the dance.

As soon as the set was finished Hester made her way swiftly to Lady Martindale without waiting to see whether her partner was following. Dungarran caught up with her just as she arrived.

'I think we've given society enough to think about for tonight,' he said. 'My self-esteem is feeling quite bruised.'

'My dear Lord Dungarran, I have hardly begun!'

'I only wish that you and my aunt were not deriving quite so much enjoyment out of it all, Miss Perceval!' He had been smiling, but he suddenly became serious. 'Ah!' he said. Hester followed his eyes. An exquisitely dressed gentleman, who had clearly just arrived, was standing in the doorway, surveying the scene. He was not above average height, but very handsome, with dark hair and eyes, and beautifully moulded mouth and chin.

Lady Martindale said softly, 'Our dear friend the Comte de Landres is here, Robert.'

'Thank you, I've seen him.' He turned to Hester and his voice had an urgent note in it as he said quietly, 'Be on your guard with the gentleman at the door. He poses as a French émigré, and is accepted everywhere in society, but his secret allegiance is to the present régime in France. He would give much to know where the French documents are, and even more to learn how much of them the War Office has managed to decipher.'

'He's coming over here, Robert.'

Dungarran said rapidly, 'Look as if you are bored beyond measure, Hester, but listen to me! The myth we have concocted will serve us very well. I know he suspects me, but he mustn't be given the slightest reason to connect you with any of it. Do you understand?'

As de Landres approached Hester turned away, saying somewhat petulantly, 'Of course I do, Lord Dungarran! Pray let us talk of something else!' She eyed the newcomer with interest as he bowed over Lady Martindale's hand.

'*Mais* Lady Martindale! How is it that you look more lovely every time I see you? The secret of eternal youth must be yours, I think…'

He would have continued in this vein but Lady Martindale smilingly interrupted. 'I see that your absence from London has not impaired your silver

tongue, monsieur! Hester, my dear, you must beware
of this gentleman. He can be charming in four different languages at once! May I present Monsieur de
Landres? Miss Perceval is at present staying with me,
monsieur, while her parents are in the north.'

'*Enchanté*, Mademoiselle Perceval.' Black eyes
surveyed her with obvious pleasure. '*Mais vraiment
enchanté!* Are you staying long in London? Please, I
beg you to say that you are!'

Hester blushed. 'You are very kind, sir. I... I'm
not yet sure...'

'Then you must give me a chance to persuade you!
Or...' The black eyes went from Hester to Dungarran.
'Am I trespassing, perhaps?'

'Oh no!' cried Hester with emphasis.

Dungarran smiled coldly. 'Miss Perceval shows little inclination to listen to anything I say, de Landres.
Perhaps you might be more successful.'

'What? Where the great Lord Dungarran has
failed? Most unlikely—but of course I will try.
Mademoiselle, may I begin by persuading you to
dance with me?'

'Thank you, I'd like to, sir.'

'Robert, you may take me to the supper room,' said
Lady Martindale. 'Hester, we shall see you there after
your dance, I hope. Meanwhile, I am sure Monsieur
de Landres will take very good care of you.'

The particular dance did not allow much opportunity for long conversations, but as they met and separated again the Comte asked any number of questions. They all demonstrated a flattering interest in

Hester and her family, and had she not been on her guard she would perhaps not have noticed how many of them involved her present association with Lady Martindale and her nephew. She took pride in the fact that her answers, apart from displaying a coolness towards Dungarran, were innocently free of any real information. The dance ended and they walked towards the supper room. The Comte returned her with a flourish to Lady Martindale and went off to find some refreshment. There seemed to be something of a crowd round the supper table. He would be some time.

'You seemed to enjoy your dance with that popinjay,' said Dungarran.

'Oh, I did!' Hester replied with a bright smile.

Dungarran frowned. 'You will remember that he's not all he seems?'

'I did. And I will.'

'What did you talk about?'

'Really, Lord Dungarran, you are as bad as he! He asked me a lot of questions, and I answered them.'

'Such as?'

'Well, some of them were flatteringly personal. But I expect you wish to know about the others. They amounted to one question really. He wanted to know what you were doing. He asked whether you spent a lot of time with the people in the War Office.'

'He must have thought you very simple, to ask outright like that.'

'You underestimate me. He did not ask outright, he was as devious as you. But that was the real question.

He also commented that you spent a great deal of time at your aunt's house.'

'What did you say to that, Hester?' asked Lady Martindale.

'I blushed and implied, without actually saying so, that Lord Dungarran's frequent visits to Grosvenor Street were on my behalf, and that his attentions were not very welcome.'

'Good!'

'But he also asked whether your nephew spent any time working on papers while he was there.'

Dungarran stared and frowned. 'The devil he did! Now I wonder how he got wind of that? What did you say?'

'I said that you were a nobleman. That you probably didn't know how to work.'

For a fraction of a moment Dungarran looked offended. Then he grinned. 'You are a minx, Hester! A cruel minx. But that was quite in the Lord Dunthinkin style!'

Hester said quickly, looking as innocent as she could, 'Lord Dunthinkin…? I've heard several people mention him. Who is he?'

Lady Martindale looked severe and shook her head at her nephew. 'Robert!'

'Oh, I'm sorry, Miss Perceval. I shouldn't have mentioned the name,' Dungarran said gravely, and only Hester could see the mocking gleam in his eye. 'He's a character in a most unsavoury book. I can't say more—it has amused my aunt, but she doesn't consider it fit for innocent girls.'

'Like most of society, Hester, I have read the book. Unlike most of the ladies of society, I even admit to having done so. But I really don't think that your parents would approve of your reading it. It is true that parts of it are extremely amusing, but much of the rest is disgusting.'

Hester was saved from further awkwardness by the return of the Comte.

At the end of the evening the conspirators all felt that their campaign had begun very well. Lady Martindale and Hester returned to Grosvenor Street in high spirits, recounting with glee the various remarks made to them by ladies whose daughters had been ignored by Dungarran in the past.

'Did you hear Lady Pembrook, Robert?' asked his fond aunt. 'She really feels for you! She complimented me on Hester's improved appearance, and added that you seemed to be quite taken with my young guest.' Lady Martindale started to laugh. 'Then, positively drooling with pleasure, she said, ''Not that I noticed any corresponding warmth in Miss Perceval's manner towards your nephew, Lady Martindale. *Au contraire!* She is distinctly cold. He has always been so successful, too... It cannot be pleasant for him.'' What do you say to that, my dear nephew?'

He looked at her in exasperation. 'That you know as well as I do that she has detested me for years. Ever since she failed in her efforts to push her unfortunate daughter into my arms, in fact. And I don't believe the poor girl even liked me!'

'Then what about Mrs Gartside?'

He sighed in resignation. 'I suppose you were listening, Godmama. You must have enjoyed that!'

'What did she say?' asked Hester.

Dungarran turned towards her. 'She was very fulsome about you. Then she said she was impressed at the change in your manner—especially towards the *eligible* young men in the room.'

'Oh!' Hester exclaimed. 'How unkind of her!'

'She is famous for her spiteful remarks. You needn't worry about her,' he said reassuringly.

'But what about the rest, Robert? Hester would like to hear that, I'm sure! Go on!'

Dungarran gave his godmother a look. Then he turned to Hester. 'I ought to tell you first that Mrs Gartside has an exquisitely lovely daughter. God knows where she got her looks from, but there's no denying that Phoebe Gartside is very beautiful. For a short while I thought I was in love with her, and the Gartsides made it very clear that they would consider me a suitable son-in-law.'

'What happened?'

'The girl has the brains of a pea! Fortunately I found this out before it was too late and withdrew. She soon found someone else—a Viscount whose intellectual gifts are on a par with her own.'

'And what did Mrs Gartside say tonight?'

'She commiserated with me! How sad it was, she said, to see a reformed flirt learning what rejection was! Even though my fortune must be such a strong temptation.'

Hester grew slightly pale. 'I was right in the first place, Lady Martindale,' she said. 'I am happier with my symbols and ciphers—they may be difficult, but they are not malicious.'

Dungarran took her hands in his. 'Hester—may I call you so in private?' She nodded. 'Hester, you mustn't let the envious spite of one or two tabbies spoil this evening. You were magnificent! Your manner towards me was perfectly judged. It is as well that I know it to be part of our game, for otherwise I would be feeling all the chagrin that those two tabbies wish on me—and more!'

Hester tried to smile, but her lips trembled. She removed her hands from his. For some unaccountable reason she suddenly felt out of spirits.

Lady Martindale looked at her sympathetically. 'Hester is tired, Robert. And if I know you both, you will be at work on your ciphers before ten o'clock tomorrow morning. It's time you left.'

Dungarran nodded, and after bidding them both goodnight he went. Lady Martindale took Hester's hand and led her to her bedroom. 'Sleep well, my dear. Robert was right. You were indeed magnificent.'

'Was she really as lovely as he said?' Hester asked sadly.

'Who?'

'The…the girl he said he loved.'

'Phoebe Gartside? Yes. She was every bit as lovely—and just as silly, too.'

'But he was in love with her. He fell in love once.'

'He was just a boy. And it lasted about a month. It wasn't real love, of course, it was pure infatuation with her looks. And as soon as he started talking to her the dream was shattered. I am sorry to say, Hester, that he has never to my knowledge been seriously in love with anyone. He has had a number of mistresses, of course. I've been told that he is a very generous lover. But properly in love? No. I doubt he ever will be—he is too...too detached.' She stole a glance at Hester. 'You are very alike, you know. Neither of you lets your heart rule your head. Isn't that true?'

'Yes!' said Hester. 'Yes! And it is better so!'

By morning Hester had recovered from her curious lack of spirits the night before. She was eager to test her new theory on the French cipher, and was already downstairs in their study when Dungarran arrived.

'You're an early bird,' he said. 'I thought I would be here first. I suppose my aunt is still in her room?'

'Yes, it was very late when we finally got to bed last night. We talked for some time after you had left.' Hester spoke absently. She was carefully drawing a figure on a piece of paper. He came over and looked at it.

'Tell me,' he said, 'how did you come to think of a pentacle?'

'Well, we both noticed a curious symmetry in the cipher—but it wasn't a circle, or a rectangle or any of the usual geometric shapes. I tried all the figures I could think of, and you did, too, but nothing seemed to work. But the pentacle is not an ordinary mathematical symbol.'

'It belongs to magic. An unusual choice for our level-headed Frenchman, surely.'

'Ah, but think of the Greek names for it!'

'One is the pentagramma, or pentagram…'

'And the other is the pentalpha. Penta alpha, Robert! Five As.'

'Because it's formed from five As! Of course! And each A would govern a different set of letters. But that would make a very complicated grid. Hours of work.'

'Exactly! But we seem to have tried all the simple ones. Let's test it! I should imagine we should quite soon see if it was working.'

After half an hour of concentrated work a coherent sentence began to appear. They looked at each other in awe.

'It's worked! It's worked, Hester! You little marvel!' An unaccustomed flush of excitement was on Dungarran's cheeks. He jumped up and dragged Hester after him. Together they danced round the room in a wild jig. At last they came to a stop by Hester's table. She went to sit down, but Dungarran put his hands on her shoulders and pulled her up against him. Hester struggled to free herself.

'No!' she protested. 'No!'

'Don't you want me to kiss you?'

'No. I don't like…kisses.'

He smiled at her, but did not release her. 'Has anyone ever kissed you before, Hester? Apart from your family?'

'You know someone has! Lord…Lord C…Canford k…kissed me. It was horrible!'

'My poor girl! That wasn't a kiss! It was an insult.'

'All the same…'

'Let me show you what a kiss can be, Hester.' His voice was persuasive, but though his hands were still on her shoulders, he was making no effort to pull her closer. 'You mustn't go through life believing that all kisses are horrible.'

'But…but surely all kisses are the same. What makes you think I should enjoy your kiss better?'

He spoke gravely, but there was a distinct twinkle in his eye. 'If you believe that all kisses are the same then it's time I taught you otherwise. I promise that you would enjoy my kiss better—I'm nicer than Lord Canford. And I think you like me more.'

'What has that got to do with it? I like working with you, talking to you—but not…not… I've never thought of…of…'

'This?' He still made no effort to draw her closer, but instead leaned forward and gently kissed her on the lips. Then he drew back and asked, 'Was that so bad? Be honest, Hester.'

'I… I don't know.' She thought for a moment. 'No, I think it…it was rather agreeable.'

'Shall I try again?' His arms slid round her and he pulled her towards him, almost imperceptibly. This time his lips met hers with more force, though he was still perfectly controlled. After a moment of panic, she felt a strange warmth taking possession of her, and she relaxed in his arms.

'Not a bit like Lord Canford,' she murmured.

He laughed and looked down at her. She smiled dreamily back at him. His expression changed, the grey eyes grew dark and she felt his arms tightening round her. This time the kiss was demanding, passionate, requiring a response. She could feel the length of his body against hers, and a wave of glorious feeling overtook her. Without volition her arms went round his neck and she returned kiss for kiss until her own body was on fire… His arms tightened till she could hardly breathe, but she rejoiced in their closeness, this strange glorious sensation fizzing along her veins like champagne…

But after a moment sanity returned to her. She pulled herself free and held on to her chair, seeking to still the trembling in her limbs. She couldn't look at him, but she heard him walk swiftly away. He was angry, it seemed. He stood by his table for a moment, and she thought she heard him cursing under his breath. Then he turned and took a step towards her. She shook her head and stammered, 'N…no more! Please! I… I…'

'Hester, for God's sake forgive me! I'm sorry! I don't know what happened! I lost my head. I can't really believe it, but it's true. I lost my head… I don't know when that last happened. I…I…' He turned away again and when he spoke his voice sounded bewildered and ashamed. 'I suppose you think me no better than Canford.'

Hester lifted her head and protested, 'Oh no! Never! You...you were very k...kind. It was my fault. I... I still don't know how to behave.'

He swung round, looking astonished. 'You really don't know what happened there, do you?' he said harshly. 'You've lived such a nun's life in that attic of yours. I very nearly lost all control! And I was supposed to be reassuring you, trying to wipe out the memory of that kiss of Canford's. I don't know what came over me. Can you possibly forgive me, Hester? I'll find it hard to forgive myself.' He came nearer. 'You are in no way to blame for what happened, believe me.'

Hester shook her head. 'Don't say any more. Please! I'd... I'd rather forget it happened.' She swallowed, and wondered if her heart would ever stop pounding. 'Can't we dismiss it from our minds? Carry on as we were before?'

His expression softened and he came towards her again. When she stiffened involuntarily, he smiled and held up his hands. 'Don't look like that. I promise you, Robert Dungarran is himself again. You're in no danger. It won't happen again, I swear.' He watched her steadily until she nodded and gave an answering smile—a little tremulous perhaps but a smile nonetheless. He went on, 'You were shocked by that last kiss, Hester. And so was I. It was not what I intended, and I agree that we should forget it. Such a triumph of emotion over reason is not our style, is it?'

Hester said wrily, 'No, indeed!'

'Then are we friends?'

When she nodded he held out a hand, and after a slight hesitation she took it. Holding it firmly in his, he said gently, 'But, all the same, you should learn a little more about life. You've been shut away in your attic for the past six years, absorbed in your figures, cut off from contact with the outside world. That's something for which I feel I share the blame. You said last night that I—Zeno—had helped to restore your confidence. Can't you let the other half of me— Robert Dungarran—teach you how to enjoy contact with the world. Confess it. You took pleasure in your success last night, didn't you?'

'Ye…es.'

'It's time you learned how much more pleasant a little light dalliance, a few light-hearted kisses between friends can be.'

'I don't think I want to try any more kisses. They're too…too unsettling.'

Lord Dungarran looked regretful. 'No kisses? Never? Not of any kind? Not even between friends?'

She said nervously, 'Well, not another like the…the last. The first two were pleasant enough. But we must get on with the transcriptions.' She sat down and pulled one of the pages towards her with determination.

He regarded her bent head with a smile in his eyes. 'You're quite right, of course. That's what we're here for.' He returned to his table, and took up his pen. After a few minutes he said thoughtfully, 'These Pentacle papers look to be quite different from the rest. Wouldn't you agree, Hester?'

'I haven't got very far, but yes, they seem to be a report on an exchange of letters...' When Lady Martindale appeared they were each busy with a bundle of papers, and once again the only noise was the scratching of pens.

In the evening they went to a less formal affair at the house of one of Lady Martindale's friends. Lowell and his friends were also invited and Hester was looking forward to relaxing in their undemanding company. Dungarran invited her as usual to the first dance, and as usual she accepted with a show of reluctance. But this time the reluctance was not completely feigned. They had worked harmoniously enough during the day, lost in the importance of the work they were doing. But outside their room, as soon as they were physically close to each other Hester remembered the feel of the tall body dominating hers that morning, her astonishingly fiery response, and she was immediately self-conscious.

'Look at me, Miss Perceval,' said Dungarran as they made their way up the set. 'I am not an ogre.'

'No, of course not. It's just that...just that...'

'You are remembering this morning, no doubt. I thought you had decided to forget it? That we were friends again.'

'It's not so easy,' replied Hester with spirit. 'I am not as used to such occurrences as you obviously are.'

For a moment they were relatively isolated at one end of the set. 'If you are talking of the first two ''occurrences'',' said Robert Dungarran, 'then I would agree with you. Age and experience make it inevitable. But the third kiss…' He shook his head with a fleeting echo of the morning's bewilderment. 'Would you believe me if I told you that I resent its effect as much as you do? It is most unlikely to happen again.'

'That, sir,' said Hester as they rejoined the progression down the set, 'is just as well!'

When the dance was over she excused herself to Lady Martindale and joined Lowell at the other end of the room with a sigh of relief. Here was someone uncomplicated, familiar and dear to her. With Lowell she could be completely herself without having to act a part or pretend. Perhaps in his company she might forget the curious ache which was rapidly developing inside her. She shook herself mentally and set her mind on enjoyment. Within minutes she was part of a laughing crowd.

'Enchanting, is she not?'

Dungarran turned. The Comte de Landres was standing at his shoulder, his eye on a figure in red and white at the other end of the room. Hester was wearing one of her muslin dresses, but had put over it a short-sleeved, wine red velvet top. Her golden head and the striking contrast of her dress were easily discernible among the young people surrounding her.

Dungarran looked at them all with a jaundiced eye. Hester had danced with her brother, then they had spent long minutes talking animatedly. After that she had turned to a friend of Lowell's with a smile and

danced with him. They had returned to the group and
started chatting again. At that point Dungarran had
decided to stop watching, and had invited an accredited beauty, one of the Season's successes, to join him
in the quadrille. The girl had twittered her way
through every movement of the dance, and he had
returned her to her chaperone when it finished with
an inward sigh of relief. But when he had looked for
Hester she was dancing with yet another green, half-
grown youth. What the devil did she see in them all?
Lowell was her brother, it was natural she should
wish to exchange a few words with him—but why
spend such a time with his friends? He was surprised,
really surprised, that Hester Perceval, who had as fine
a mind as he had ever met, should wish to waste her
time on such lightweights. He had half a mind to go
down there and ask her to dance with him again. It
would at least remove him from de Landres's presence. But after a moment's thought he decided not to.
It would be too painful if she refused him in front of
all those striplings. And she almost certainly would—
because of their damned pretence, of course!

De Landres looked at him with knowing amusement. 'She seems remarkably happy with those young
people.'

'One of them is her brother, de Landres.'

'Ah! That accounts for it. And I daresay she finds
them something of a relief after the rarefied atmosphere of Grosvenor Street. How is your work on ciphers progressing?'

Dungarran turned and gave him a cool stare. 'Ciphers?'

'I hear you are an expert, milord. Everyone at the Horse Guards sings the praises of Zeno.'

'Come, you are trying to flatter me. I dabble in mathematics under the name of Zeno, you're quite right there. But ciphers?'

'I heard about the lecture at the New…what was it again? The New Scientific and Philosophical Society. Did you ever trace your Euclid?'

'Er…no. That young man seems to have disappeared completely.'

'A pity. Apparently he was an enthusiast. He could have been a great help to you,' said de Landres sympathetically. 'It's a slow business working alone.'

Dungarran examined the Frenchman with cool disapproval. 'Working? I don't know what you mean. You're obviously confusing me with someone else.'

'Come, milord! Why do you try to fob me off like this?' de Landres said gently. 'It's common knowledge at the War Office that Zeno, alias Dungarran, is deciphering some documents stolen from the French. Am I not right? There's nothing wrong in my knowing that, surely? I am as eager as anyone to see the tyrant Napoleon defeated. What are they? Reports on supplies?'

Dungarran eyed him grimly. It was obvious that some idiot at the War Office was being far too indiscreet with someone he thought was an ally. De Landres's true allegiance—to Napoleon—was still unknown to all but a few.

'Your friends at the War Office may well be prepared to broadcast their secrets to the world, sir. I am not.'

'Such discretion! But I wonder why you find it necessary to work at Lady Martindale's house rather than your own? Can it be that you are letting yourself be…distracted by her young visitor? Is that why the task is proceeding so slowly? Or is that because the ciphers are too difficult?'

'Are these French ways, de Landres? I have to say that, in an Englishman, I would find such curiosity, such questions about my deeper feelings, damned impertinent! We will not discuss Miss Perceval, if you please.'

'As you wish, Dungarran. But I warn you, I shall carry on asking questions of my friend at the War Office.'

'And who is that?'

'What? And have you order him to keep a watch on his tongue? No, no! You will have to find that out for yourself, *milord*!' He bowed and walked away with a self-assurance which Dungarran found immensely irritating.

Chapter Ten

If Dungarran had only known, Hester was finding her brother's company less amusing than she had expected. Lowell had begun by introducing her to Mr Woodford Gaines.

'How nice to meet you, sir,' she said. 'But I thought you were in Devon with your godfather?'

'Indeed I am, Miss Perceval! That is to say, I'm not with him at the moment, but I was till yesterday. And I shall go back to him quite soon. I came up to town to try to persuade old Lowers to join me, don't y'know. Dashed boring in Devon with only a godfather for company! He wants to walk or play chess all the time!'

'Lowers? Oh, you mean my brother!' She gave Lowell a sisterly look. 'And has Mr Gaines persuaded you, Lowell?'

Lowell, looking rather uncomfortable, said, 'I was going to tell you, Hes. I'm off with Gaines the day after tomorrow. You'll be all right, though, won't you? I know it means that you're on your own in

London, now that Hugo has gone back with Pa and Ma. But they were happy to leave you with Lady Martindale. And Dungarran is there. He'll keep an eye on you.'

Hester kept her voice even. 'You know what I think of Lord Dungarran, Lowell.'

'I thought that had all changed? He seems to be pretty nutty on you now!'

'That doesn't mean to say that I am "nutty" on him!' she replied sharply. Then she relented and spoke as warmly as she could. 'Of course I shall be all right. Lady Martindale is very kind to me.' She gave him an ironic look. 'And I am sure you'll enjoy walking and playing chess in Totnes.'

The two young men burst into laughter. 'The old man has a nap in the afternoon and goes to bed at ten, Miss Perceval,' cried Mr Gaines. 'And the cider is strong and plentiful in Devon.'

'From what I hear, so are the barmaids, eh, Gaines?' The two gave another roar of laughter. Hester was not particularly amused. She had not seen a great deal of Lowell since she had joined Lady Martindale, but he had always been there in the background, a reassuring family presence. Now she would be the only Perceval left in the capital. Lowell saw her disquiet and tried to make amends.

'Come and dance, Sis.' As they walked on to the floor he said, 'If you're really upset I won't go. It's just that Gaines was so keen to have my company, and…and you seemed to be quite settled with Lady

Martindale…and Dungarran.' He gave her a sideways
look. 'I've hardly seen you for days.'

As they danced Hester wrestled with the temptation
to tell him the truth. But was she sure what the truth
was? She had been blackmailed into a reluctant working relationship with Dungarran, that was true. It was
also true that his present admiration for her was
feigned, put on purely for the benefit of society. Even
Lowell had no idea that it was merely a ruse, a device
to enable her to continue working with Dungarran
without rousing comment. But…how had this morning's events affected that 'working relationship'?
Those kisses had surely not been in the plan…

Lowell was worried by her silence. 'Shall I not go,
Hester? Shall I stay in London?'

'No, no!' Hester made up her mind. The secret of
her deciphering work was not hers to reveal. It was
tempting to confide in Lowell, especially as he obviously felt neglected, but she must not. She must
keep up the pretence.

'No, you must go with Mr Gaines,' she said firmly.
'I confess I have qualms about the strong cider, but
the barmaids, being equally strong, will keep you both
in order, no doubt. No, Lowell, you mustn't give up
your trip for my sake. I am very happy with Lady
Martindale, she is a delightful hostess. But I hope
you'll be here to escort me back to Abbot Quincey
when the time comes?'

'Oh, I will! I'll be back well before then! Er…that
is to say…when were you thinking of going, Hester?'

Hester experienced a strange reluctance to name a

day. The deciphering of the documents could not possibly take longer than another two weeks. But to state in so many words that she would leave Grosvenor Street so soon, say goodbye to Lady Martindale and her nephew… 'I… I'm not sure,' she said. 'We must both be back home by the middle of next month.'

'For the July fête—'

'And Hugo's birthday.'

'But that's a long time ahead.'

'It doesn't seem so long to me,' said Hester, perhaps more sadly than she realised.

They danced in silence for a while. Then Lowell said, 'Perhaps Dungarran would come to Abbot Quincey for the fête?'

'Robert Dungarran? The perfect London gentleman? Come to a country fête, complete with farmers, sideshows, Morris dancers and bucolic merriment all round? Don't be silly, Lowell!'

'Then perhaps for Hugo's birthday? That's only a day or two later.'

'Why on earth should he? I neither expect him nor want him!'

'I was only thinking he was Hugo's friend,' said Lowell meekly. 'Nothing to do with you, of course, Sis.'

Hester gave her brother a sharp glance. 'Well, he isn't! Don't start imagining things, Lowell.'

Her brother said no more, but since he was a kind person at heart he exerted himself to distract her, and when the dance ended and they returned to his friends he made sure that Hester never lacked a partner.

His efforts were appreciated when Hester observed Dungarran dancing with a ravishingly beautiful, dark-haired girl dressed in pale pink. He was looking down at her, his head bent in its familiar pose, an indulgent smile on his face. The mysterious pain inside Hester was suddenly so acute that she had difficulty in breathing.

'Hes! What is it? What's the matter?' Lowell's voice seemed to come from a long way off. She conquered her malaise with an effort and forced a smile.

'I... I...don't know. It suddenly felt stuffy in here. I'm all right now.'

'You went whiter than your dress. Are you sure you're all right?'

'Yes, yes, please don't make a fuss, Lowell. It was nothing. I... I think I should go back to Lady Martindale. She will be wondering where I am.'

'Don't worry! Her nephew will reassure her. He's hardly taken his eyes off you ever since you joined us.'

'Really?' asked Hester, with a glance at the couples now leaving the floor. 'I find that very difficult to believe!' Dungarran was totally absorbed in ushering his partner tenderly towards the chaperones' corner. He was bowing over her hand and the silly girl was looking completely enchanted... Hester pulled herself together. She would not look at them, she would not! She turned and smiled brilliantly at Mr Gaines. 'If you are depriving me of Lowell's company for the next week or so, Mr Gaines, you may console me with the next dance!'

Mr Gaines went scarlet with embarrassed pleasure. 'Miss Perceval! What an honour! No, I mean it!'

The return to Grosvenor Street was by no means as merry as that of the night before. Dungarran seemed preoccupied, and though Hester talked gaily to Lady Martindale about Lowell and his friends, it was evident that she was not as happy as she pretended. Lady Martindale looked from one to the other and grew thoughtful, but she waited until they were in the house again before she spoke.

'What did de Landres have to say, Robert? Whatever it was, you were both quite absorbed.'

'He worries me. He asked again about the ciphers, and made no attempt to disguise his curiosity—nor to hide the fact that he knew a great deal about them already.'

'Do you think he knows that you suspect him?' asked Hester.

'I am sure he doesn't. It's more that he is desperate to know how fast we are progressing, and especially whether I have any assistance. He mentioned Euclid, but I told him the young man had disappeared.'

'Which is no more than the truth,' said Lady Martindale with a smile. She grew serious and went on slowly, 'It must be important to him. He took quite a risk in showing how much he knew. I wonder who his informant is?'

'Some sprig of the nobility with more pedigree than brains. There are several such in the Horse Guards. It won't be difficult to find and deal with him. But de Landres is a different matter…'

'I wonder why he is in such a hurry?' asked Hester. 'It's almost as if a time is important to him.'

'I agree. Of course, timing is always important in military campaigns. But I would be surprised if his concern is about the French supply lines in Eastern Europe; if he knows as much as I think he does, he knows that keeping that information from the Allies is a lost cause—those documents have already been deciphered and sent off.'

'It must be something to do with the Pentacle papers! But what? We've only just started on them.'

'Then we'll have to work longer hours, Hester! We'll start earlier in the mornings.'

'You're a slave-driver, Robert!' protested Lady Martindale. 'The poor girl works hard enough! She is in London chiefly for the Season, don't forget! She's supposed to be enjoying herself.'

Hester thought of the party they had just attended. It would be no pleasure to her to watch while Robert Dungarran indulged in more of his light-hearted flirtations with lovely young girls. 'I think I enjoy my ciphers more, Lady Martindale. I know I am odd, but to me they are still far more fascinating than the…than the dances and courtesies of the polite world.'

'I'm not sure your parents would be pleased, however! And what about your brother?'

'Lowell is leaving London for a while. He is joining Mr Gaines in Devon.'

'Ah, Mr Gaines! The fellow with the useful wardrobe, and a godfather in Totnes! I had quite forgotten him,' said Dungarran.

'What are you talking about, Robert?'

'An earlier episode in my acquaintance with the Perceval family. But I digress. You were accusing me of being a slave-driver, I think.'

'Hester seems to be reconciled to it. However, I hope you will leave our evenings free. Or are you going to keep her prisoner here till the Pentacle papers are done?'

'I don't have to, Aunt. As Hester has said, the difficulty is to teach her to appreciate, even to enjoy, the pleasures of society. I have no intention of reducing her opportunities for light-hearted dalliance—quite the contrary. But I don't believe starting earlier on the ciphers will disturb her.'

'Then we must all go to bed right now!' Lady Martindale said briskly. 'It's very late, and you will both be at your tables long before I am up—as you were this morning. I hope your parents never learn what a poor sort of chaperone I am, Hester. But there! They don't know my nephew as I do. You are as safe with him as you would be with me. In spite of what he has just said, I know that the work you do together is far more important to him than any light-hearted dalliance.'

It was as well that she was already halfway out of the door, and so did not see the scarlet flooding Hester's cheeks and her nephew's slightly self-conscious look.

* * *

When Hester entered the study early the next morning she found Dungarran already hard at work.

'Have you been to bed at all?' she asked in astonishment.

'Good morning.' He got up and took her hand in his. 'For a short while. There's a possibility that I may have to go to Portsmouth later. A note was waiting for me when I got back last night.'

'Portsmouth! But you can't! We have work to do here!'

'I know we have work to do, and I've told the Admiralty so. But I may not have any choice. I'm still waiting to hear what they decide.' At her sigh of exasperation he went on, 'It's connected with the work we've been doing, Hester. Some fool of an Admiral wants me to explain parts of our transcription to his captains before they set sail for the Baltic.'

'But…but what about the Pentacle papers? Aren't they important, too?'

'Of course they are! So shall we get down to them?'

Hester sat down at the table without replying. At first she found it difficult to settle, but after a short while she was fascinated once again by the sentences gradually unfolding before her eyes. When the messenger came with word for Dungarran she was surprised to see that they had been working for two hours. It was half past ten.

'I'm sorry, Hester,' he said after reading the note.

'I have to go after all. But I ought to be back in three or four days.'

'Three or four days!'

'I assure you I'll finish there as quickly as I can.' He took her hand. 'You'll miss me?'

'Of course I will!' she said and snatched her hand away. 'I shall have to work twice as hard!'

'I have no doubt that you will!' He grew serious. 'Avoid conversation with de Landres. The time is coming when we shall have to do something about that gentleman, but meanwhile he mustn't have the slightest suspicion of your involvement. Promise?'

She cast a glance at the papers strewn on the table. 'I don't think I'll have time for conversations with anyone! Yes, I promise.'

'Then I shall leave you. But…before I go… Have we time for a little—a very little—light-hearted dalliance, would you say?' He took her hand again and pulled her closer. A kiss, light as a feather, touched her lips. 'A reminder,' he said softly. 'So that you don't forget our agreement.'

'A…agreement?'

'I promised to teach you the pleasure of kisses between friends, remember?' He observed the rosy colour in her cheeks with satisfaction and kissed her hand. 'It's time I went!'

But halfway to the door he stopped, came back and kissed her again, this time more comprehensively. Once more the blood ran through her veins like fire and she would have responded just as passionately as the day before, if she had not exerted every ounce of self-control. His arms tightened, and he kissed her again. Then he slowly let his arms fall and gave a short laugh.

'You must be a witch! Given time, I think you could prove my aunt wrong. Goodbye, Hester!' He was gone.

Hester was left staring at the door. What had he meant? Lady Martindale had said that his work was more important to him than light-hearted dalliance. Did that mean...? Hester put her hand to her throat. Then she shook her head as if to clear it. Given time, he had said... There was her answer. Robert Dungarran would never give himself time to fall in love, never!... Fall in love? Where had that idea come from? Hester Perceval was not interested whether Robert Dungarran fell in love or not! Falling in love was not in her own plan for the future! She turned with determination to the Pentacle papers.

Lady Martindale came in a little later looking worried. 'Hester, this trip of Robert's is very annoying! He's away for three, perhaps even four days! And I've promised to go out to Richmond to spend the day with an old friend on Monday. That's only the day after tomorrow. Shall I postpone my visit? Or would you like to come with me?'

'You're very kind, but I don't think I could do that, Lady Martindale. Now that your nephew has disappeared off to Portsmouth it's more than ever important that one of us is working!'

Lady Martindale smiled. 'Robert's work in

Portsmouth is just as important, my dear. For some reason or other the people there don't trust anyone else as much. They regard him as indispensable.'

'Oh. Well, in view of what we said last night about urgency I shall be fully occupied with these!' Hester made a gesture to the papers on the table. 'But please don't postpone your visit for my sake. I shan't have time to feel lonely!'

'I would prefer not to disappoint her...' said Lady Martindale, still a little undecided. 'She's an invalid and doesn't have many visitors... Are you sure you won't come with me?'

'Quite sure! In fact, if on Monday you could tell your servants to say there is no one at home, that would suit me even more. I'd like to work undisturbed.'

'Of course! Most of them have leave to be out in the afternoon, so you should have complete quiet.'

Apart from meals and a walk in the park insisted on by Lady Martindale, Hester worked quietly and steadily the next day. She was aware of feeling slightly lost, of missing the tall figure at the other table, and if she had allowed herself the indulgence, she would have been miserable. But the work became more and more absorbing. Unlike the previous documents which had all concerned supply lines to the army throughout Europe, the Pentacle papers summarised an exchange of letters between Paris and the French command in Spain. At first they dealt with the demands made by Napoleon on his generals in the

Peninsula, demands which the men on the ground clearly regarded as unrealistic. Later, however, the sentences grew more veiled. They seemed to be hinting at a plot of some kind… Lady Martindale had difficulty in prising her away for an early night.

When Lady Martindale came in to bid her goodbye the next morning Hester was already totally absorbed in her papers.

'I'm still not sure I should leave you like this. You'll work yourself into a brainstorm.'

Hester looked up blankly, then rose and took off her glasses. 'Dear Lady Martindale, I shall be perfectly happy working away here. In Northamptonshire I often spent hours alone in my attic and loved every minute of it. Enjoy your visit to your friend and forget me.'

'Very well. But promise me that if you feel tired you will take a short walk! Bertram would go with you. Make sure you take him! I shall see you tonight, my dear.'

The house was indeed quiet after Lady Martindale had gone, but Hester laboured on without noticing. It was becoming clear that the plot concerned an assassination attempt. But whose? Obviously someone important—the letters described him as one of Napoleon's greatest enemies. Hester sat back in thought. Who was this person? She suddenly sat up again and stared at the papers before her. Could it possibly be *Wellington*? He was in Spain at the moment and his recent campaign in the Peninsula had posed practically the only successful resistance in the whole of Europe to the Emperor's armies. But there had so far been no mention of a name. She bent over her work again.

But by mid-afternoon her back was stiff and her head was aching. After she had made several stupid mistakes she decided that the short walk required by Lady Martindale was called for. Apart from Bertram, an elderly footman at the door, the house seemed devoid of servants. They were clearly taking advantage of Lady Martindale's absence to have a day's freedom. Hester fetched her hat and went out, waving away Bertram's offer to accompany her. She murmured something about going to see her brother and this seemed to satisfy him. But once outside, her feet turned as if by instinct in the direction of Hatchard's, and soon she was on her way past the table of new books in the front of the shop to the shelves on mathematics. She would just snatch a quick look before returning… She froze when she heard a familiar voice, and drew back behind a tall bookcase.

'Well, Behring, what do you have for me today?' said the Comte de Landres. 'Have the new French classics arrived? No? A pity! I'll have a look through the shelves over there, however. I may have missed a treasure the last time I looked.' Hester leaned further back. She had no wish to meet the Comte. There was silence for a moment, then de Landres's voice could be heard just on the other side of the shelves. Someone else had joined him. They were speaking softly and in rapid French, but Hester, suspicious now, could hear every word.

'Did you find anything?'

'Nothing at all.'

'Then the papers can't be at Curzon Street. And they aren't anywhere at the Horse Guards, either. It is as I thought, they must be in the Martindale house. Probably in the small room on the right.'

'What do you want us to do?'

'The timing could not be better! With Dungarran in Portsmouth and the two women in Richmond for the day, the house is empty.'

'Servants?'

'All out, except for one footman. He's old, Armand could easily deal with him. No need to hurt him. Where did you leave Armand, by the way?'

'I took him back to the inn. He's safer there. He can't speak English, and he's doesn't exactly look the gentleman. So—what do you want us to do? Bring the papers to you?'

'No. It's very risky, but I think I'll join you in Grosvenor Street. I want to be sure we get the right papers. I can't read the things but I'll recognise them—and the sooner they're burnt the better. That's vital. If anything should go wrong, if we're caught, those papers must be destroyed—understood?'

'We won't get caught.'

'Get rid of the papers!'

'All right, all right! I understand. I'd best be on my way. I have to collect Armand.'

'When will you be at the house?'

'In an hour. Less, perhaps.'

'I'll call there in an hour. I can pretend to be visiting, if necessary.'

Hester waited until de Landres had followed his accomplice out of the shop, and then she scurried out. The Pentacle papers were in danger and she must rescue them! De Landres's desperation to get rid of them before they could be deciphered proved their importance. Hardly knowing what she would do, she half walked, half ran back to Grosvenor Street. The door was shut but not locked, and the footman was nowhere to be seen. He was old and lazy—he had probably decided to have a rest, leaving the door unlocked in case she came back sooner than expected. Inside the study she gathered up the papers and the notes she had been making and stuffed them all into Lady Martindale's sewing bag, which was on the floor by her chair. She looked round frantically. Her glasses! They were lying on the table. She snatched them up and hurried out again, not quite knowing where she was going, only desperate to put as great a distance as possible between herself and the house in Grosvenor Street. Lowell! She would find Lowell. Halfway to Half Moon Street she stopped dead. Lowell wouldn't be there! He had left for Devon with Woodford Gaines, and the house would be empty. Her heart sank. But after a moment's thought she rallied again. Mr Gaines's servant knew her. If he was still there he would let her in. She might find an hour's refuge there—enough time, at least, to decide what to do next. Oh, *why* was Dungarran so far away just when she needed him most? How could she keep the Pentacle papers out of the hands of de Landres for another two days? She hurried on…

But Dungarran in fact returned earlier than expected from Portsmouth. He had finished his business there without ceremony, finding that half the captains he had been required to speak to were already at sea. Cursing the inefficient dotards at the Admiralty, he had set off early, wasting no time on the road. He used the importance of deciphering the Pentacle papers to explain his urgent desire to be back in London, but as he drew nearer to the capital, he had to acknowledge to himself that he was equally impatient to see Hester Perceval again. Try as he might to dismiss the feeling as irrational and illogical, it simply would not go away. He was more than a little irritated by this lack of control over his emotions. It didn't help that he found himself making for Grosvenor Street instead of his own home. His aunt and Hester would be out at a soirée, but he could wait for them there, and meanwhile examine what Hester had been doing on the papers.

He reached Grosvenor Street just after eleven o'clock, but he arrived at a household in chaos.

'Robert! Oh, thank God you're here!' Lady Martindale's normal air of self-possession had vanished and she clutched her nephew's arm with desperate fingers. 'Hester has vanished!'

'What?'

'She's gone! And that's not all. So have the papers!'

'To hell with the papers. *What has happened to Hester?*'

'She sent this note.' Lady Martindale looked round distractedly and produced a crumpled piece of paper. Dungarran smoothed it out and took it to the window. He let out a long breath.

'It is her writing,' he said. 'I recognise it. And she says she is safe.'

'But where is she? Bertram saw her go out about three o'clock this afternoon and she hasn't been seen since. That's nearly eight hours ago!'

'Where did the note come from?'

'The servants tell me it was delivered just before I returned—by someone they didn't recognise.'

'Man or woman?'

'A man. But they were in such a state themselves that they didn't really notice anything more about him.'

'Why? What happened, Godmama? Why did Hester go?'

'That's what I was trying to tell you. The house has been ransacked, Robert! While I was out at Richmond two men broke in, bundled Bertram into a cupboard—he could have died of suffocation for all they cared!—and searched the place for your papers. They made such a mess… Come and see.'

Dungarran looked round grimly at the devastation in the study. His face twisted as he saw on the floor a bright blue apron, spotted with ink. He picked it up and stared at it for a moment. Then he said as if to reassure both his aunt and himself, 'The note said she was safe. Was she here when the men came?'

'I don't know! Bertram says not. He says she went out long before they appeared. But...'

'Well?'

'He's certain she wasn't carrying anything.'

'No papers. Did she have anyone with her—a footman? No, of course not! Did she say where she was going?'

'Bertram thinks she said she was going to see her brother.'

'And he didn't see her return?'

'He is a little evasive, Robert. I think he left the door unattended for a while—he sometimes does when left to himself, and she might have come in then. But he is quite sure he didn't hear her voice while the two men were here. Surely she would have made some protest?'

'She has spirit—she would have protested a great deal!' He looked at the apron. 'Unless she was hurt?'

Lady Martindale sat down suddenly. 'Robert! Oh no!'

He took a deep breath and said firmly, 'We must believe that she wasn't here. Let me think about that note...' After a pause he said slowly, 'Hester must have left before the intruders arrived—she says the papers are safe. That means she had time to gather them up and take them with her.'

'I suppose so... What I don't understand is why she took them at all! How could she have known in advance that the men were coming?' Lady Martindale put her hands to her head. 'But if she didn't know, why did she run away? I shall go mad, Robert! It goes round and round in my brain till I can't think at all! And in spite of the note and what you and Bertram say, I'm so worried about Hester. Where on earth can she be?'

'What have you done so far?' Dungarran's voice was still calm. Only his knuckles, white against the blue apron, betrayed his tension.

'I thought she might have gone home, so I sent every man I could find round all the inns with coaches for the north. No one has hired a coach for Northampton since last Friday, and no one answering Hester's description travelled on the Mail or any of the stage coaches. The fellow at the ticket office said there were no women at all on the Mail tonight. He noticed particularly.'

'What else?'

'There hasn't been time for much else, but one of the maids says that she saw Hester crossing Berkeley Square. I wondered if she had gone round to see Lowell, as Bertram had said. I was just about to send someone to ask.'

'I'll go,' Dungarran said brusquely. 'It won't take long.'

But when he roused the sleepy manservant in Half Moon Street he was informed that Mr Perceval had left London that afternoon for Devon.

'Accompanied?'

'Mr Gaines went the day before yesterday, my lord.'

'But was there no one else with Mr Perceval?'

The manservant looked puzzled. 'I cannot say. I was out at the time. He was here this morning when I left, but the house was empty when I got back at about eight o'clock. Mr Gaines allows me to visit my mother on the last Monday of the month, my lord,' he added, a touch defensively.

Dungarran rewarded the man and returned to Grosvenor Street. 'That must be where she's gone, Aunt! With Lowell to Totnes!' The apron was folded over again and tucked inside his pocket.

'Totnes? But why—oh, of course! Devon. Lowell was to join Mr Gaines there. That must be it… Robert! Where are you going?'

'To Curzon Street. I'll pick up my man and be off to Devon within the hour.'

'But you've only just come back from Portsmouth. You must have some kind of rest! It's almost two days' journey to Totnes!'

Lord Dungarran came back into the room and took his aunt's hands in his. 'I shan't rest until I know where Hester is. And if she has those papers the matter is all the more urgent.' He made to go again, but Lady Martindale held him back.

'What can I do to help?'

'Make sure that our friend the Comte de Landres doesn't follow me!'

'How can I do that?'

'Get some of your friends at the War Office to arrest him. He must be behind this.'

Chapter Eleven

Robert was back in three days, but he had no good news. Mr Gaines's godfather was seriously ill and Lowell Perceval's plan to spend time with his friend in Devon had been abandoned the day after it was formed. So far as Woodford Gaines knew, Lowell had never left London.

'So we are none the wiser?' said Lady Martindale anxiously.

Her nephew shook his head. 'I haven't seen a trace of either of the Percevals. What about de Landres? Does he know anything?'

'He's been questioned. He admits he engaged the men to search for the papers, but claims that they didn't find them. He has even admitted that he was there himself. But there was no sign of Hester,' he said. 'Except for Bertram the house was deserted. And while I wouldn't believe a word the villain said, Bertram confirms it. He still thinks Hester went out to visit her brother. And now both Percevals are missing! What are we to make of it?' Lady Martindale walked up and down in agitation, hardly able to suppress tears. 'Robert, I shall soon have to send a message to Sir James and Lady Perceval! What am I to say?'

Dungarran's face was lined with worry and fatigue, but he said firmly, 'Wait a little. We don't wish to give them an unnecessary fright. Wherever they are, I believe Hester and Lowell are together. We must hope so, at least. If she *did* know that de Landres was coming to steal the papers—'

'How *could* she?'

'I don't know, Godmama, but it's the only thing that explains her behaviour.' Hearing the impatient irritation in his voice, he endeavoured to speak more calmly. 'She took the papers to a place where de Landres couldn't find them, and she got her brother to help her. She must be somewhere we haven't thought of. I think we should have another talk with the servant in the house in Half Moon Street. Come, Godmama!'

Together they went to Half Moon Street. Here they found the manservant very ready to talk. He reiterated that he had seen neither Hester nor Lowell, but he told them of two used brandy glasses he had found since talking to Dungarran, and taking him to one side he said softly, 'I don't like to mention it before her ladyship, but there was women's clothing in Mr Lowell's chamber, too. I've folded it up but it's still there.'

'Fetch it, man!'

When he brought it down Lady Martindale exclaimed, 'Why, that's Hester's dress!' She looked fearfully at her nephew. 'W...What does it mean?'

For the first time since coming back from Portsmouth Robert Dungarran's features relaxed. 'Not what you fear, Godmama. In fact, I think I know now what the Percevals have done and where they are.' He thanked the manservant suitably, and took his aunt home.

'If you will write a note for Lady Perceval I shall deliver it in person. But I think... I hope it will not be needed.'

'You know where they are? But how?'

'They are almost certainly in Northamptonshire.'

'How could they have got there? We enquired...'

'After a young lady. Do you remember that Hester Perceval once attended a lecture in St James's Square?'

'Dressed as a young man! Of course! Those clothes of hers... She changed her clothes in Half Moon Street. Oh Robert! I think that must be the answer. And what a clever disguise!'

'I shall have to go straight away. I think they are safe in their own home, but I won't be at ease until I see them there.'

'Yes, yes! Shall I come with you?'

'I'm not sure you would enjoy the rate at which I propose to travel, Aunt.'

'Then you must send a message back as soon as you know! I shall be on the rack until I hear from you. Oh, Robert, I pray with all my heart you are right!'

Robert looked at his aunt's face. Lady Martindale had aged by ten years in the last week. Her cheeks were pale and dark circles lay under her eyes. Her hands were trembling. He took one in his and pressed it comfortingly.

'They are! I know they are!' he said gently, putting as much assurance into his voice as he could. 'And I shall send a message telling you so. Trust me.'

Dungarran travelled overnight in a hired chaise and four. His activities of the last week caught up with him and, in spite of his worries, he finally fell asleep. But his slumbers were fitful and broken by nightmares and nameless fears. He was not as certain that Hester was at Abbot Quincey as he had led his aunt to believe. But if not, where else would he look? The note said she was safe, but was she? The thought that she might be in the hands of strangers, with only Lowell to help her, was torture. He was incapable of rational thought, unable to persuade himself that, logically, he was very likely to find Hester comfortably installed in her own home, engaged in the further decipherment of the Pentacle papers. Strangely, none of his anxieties were for those same papers. All his thoughts were for Hester.

Daylight restored him to something of his former self. He started planning what he should do. It was too early to go to Perceval Hall, nor was he in a state to call on anyone. He must find somewhere to repair the damage of five days' almost continuous travel. At the first likely-looking inn he ordered the coachman to stop, and asked his man to step inside and order a room. The landlord was just stirring and was astonished at being asked to provide a room at what seemed to him to be the wrong end of the night.

'Do you have a room?' Wicklow asked coldly.

'Oh yes, sir. Several.'

'Then we shall take the best. His lordship would like breakfast in half an hour. But first we should like plenty of hot water and towels.' Then as the man stared he added, 'As soon as possible!'

Aided by Wicklow, Dungarran made himself more respectable. He washed and shaved, then put on a clean shirt and cravat. His coat was shaken and brushed, and his boots polished, though not altogether to his man's satisfaction. The breakfast was a hearty one, and Dungarran made himself eat a fair amount. However impatient he was, he must try to be sensible. The next hour or two might very well be a testing time. At last the hour was sufficiently advanced for Dungarran to be received at Perceval Hall. Outwardly his usual imperturbable, well-dressed self, he got in the coach once again and gave the order to drive off.

As he approached Hester's home the beauty of the house and grounds made no impression on him. It was taking all his considerable strength of character to retain an air of polite calm, and presenting himself and his mission to the Percevals in a reasonable manner would test every social skill he possessed. He did not know what he would do if Hester were not here…

The door opened as the coach came to a halt.

'Good morning. My name is Dungarran. Are Sir

James and Lady Perceval at home?' He went in and waited in the entrance hall while the servant disappeared to consult. Of course they were at home! It was a ridiculously early hour to call—any sensible person would still be at breakfast, or in bed… Perhaps it would have been better to ask for Hugo? Less conventional, but safer… What a time the wretched man was taking!… He strode restlessly up and down the hall, stopping before a portrait of a young lady dressed in the clothes of the previous century, where he tried to trace a similarity to Hester. What would he do if she were not here?

'Will you come this way, please?'

He followed the servant into a small parlour. Lady Perceval was sitting by the window. Sir James, looking rather puzzled, came forward to meet him.

'Good morning, Dungarran. Er…what can I do for you? Did you wish to see Hugo? He's just coming…'

'No, Sir James. It was you I wanted to see.'

'Of course! How stupid of me! You've brought a message from my daughter! How is she? And Lady Martindale? Both well, I hope?'

Lady Perceval came over to him. 'How very kind of you, Lord Dungarran! Though I was rather hoping to see Hester before too long. We miss her, you know.'

An icy hand was clutching Dungarran's throat, making it impossible for him to speak. Hester was not, after all, here. His worst fears, the fears he had refused to give way to, had been realised.

The silence was broken by Hugo, who came striding into the room, a broad smile on his face and his hand outstretched. 'Robert! What the devil are you doing here? It's damned good to see you! Can you stay?'

The moment could not be put off any longer. Dungarran took Lady Martindale's letter out of his pocket and handed it to Sir James. 'I…I'm sorry, sir,' he said.

Lady Perceval turned to her husband. 'What is it? What is it, James? Something's wrong! It's Hester!' He was busy with the letter and didn't hear her. She turned again to Dungarran. 'Is she ill?'

Sir James led her gently back to her seat. After a quick look Hugo came over to sit next to her. 'I'm afraid it's bad news, my dear. Lady Martindale tells us that Hester is missing. She has not been seen for…' He took out his glasses and looked at the letter again. 'Nearly five days?' His voice expressed shock and growing anger. Lady Perceval gave a little scream.

'You don't mean it! You can't mean that Hester…my darling— No, no! It can't be!' Hugo put his arms round her, but she shook him off. 'Your aunt promised to look after her!' she cried to Dungarran. 'I trusted her! What happened? What can possibly have happened?'

Dungarran was white but he remained calm. 'I was in Portsmouth, and Lady Martindale was visiting a friend in Richmond. My aunt had urged Miss Perceval to go with her, but she refused. I am aware that it was very wrong of us to leave her alone, but she was insistent that she wanted to carry on with…with some work she had been doing. As far as we can tell she left the house of her own accord, taking the…the work with her.' He turned to Sir James. 'We thought we knew where she was, Sir James. As soon as I returned to London and heard what had happened I went straight down to Devon in search of her. But we were wrong. I've since wasted no time in coming here. She…she left this note with one of Lady Martindale's servants.' He handed over the scrap of paper—the only source of hope. His hand trembling, Sir James took it and read it out.

'"I am quite safe and so are the papers.—Hester."' He looked up. 'But this was four nights ago? And not another word from her since? Good God, man, what can have happened to her?'

Dungarran's lips tightened. 'I…I don't know,' he said.

Hugo cried angrily, 'Don't stand there saying you don't know! Why aren't you out there looking for her? Father, if you don't mind I'll collect my things and set off straight away for London. Hester must be there somewhere.'

'We think Lowell is almost certainly with her,' said Dungarran. 'There is some evidence for it.'

There was a shocked silence, then Hugo said, 'He can't be. Lowell can't be with her. He's here. I've just been out for a ride with him.'

'Heavens above, Lord Dungarran! Where is my daughter?' cried Lady Perceval in great distress.

'Yes, Dungarran,' said Sir James grimly. 'Where is Hester now?'

'Here, Papa,' said a new voice. Everyone turned. Hester Perceval stood in the doorway, one hand clutching the doorframe, the other holding a sheaf of papers.

After a moment's stunned silence the family converged on the door. Mother and father, Hugo, even Lowell, who had followed his sister into the room, hugged Hester in turn, exclaiming, laughing, admonishing, expressing their delight that she was safe.

Dungarran took one long look at the figure in the doorway, then went over to the window, leaving the Percevals to rejoice among themselves. Ordinary courtesy would demand that he left them to their jubilations unwatched by an outsider. But it was not anything so conventional as courtesy that had moved him to stand with his back to the room, staring at the landscape outside. He had a battle to fight unseen. Never before had he been subject to such a riot of feelings as was now threatening to overwhelm him. His famous detachment had in the past carried him through many a dramatic situation with no loss of dignity or control. Now it had deserted him. Nothing in his life had disturbed him so much as the sight of Hester Perceval in that doorway.

He put his hands against the window-pane in an effort to absorb its coolness into his blood. He was struggling against a primitive urge to snatch the girl into his arms, to hold her so passionately close that she could hardly breathe, to carry her off to some remote island where they could live for ever and lose all sight of the world... At the same time he felt an absurd tenderness, a desire to cherish her, protect from all harm, to throw away the hideous clothes she was wearing and replace them with lace and satin and jewels, to demonstrate to the wide world his pride and joy in her...

But at war with both of these was a growing anger. How *dare* she subject him to such anxiety! If she had thought half as much of him as he of her, she would have sent a message before now to reassure him! The thought of his fruitless journeys, the long road to Devon and back, the nightmares of the night before, enraged him beyond measure. How *dare* she have so little consideration for his feelings! How *dare* she have taken such a hold on his heart that he had lost all sense! The coolly logical mind, in which he had taken such pride, was now, thanks to this woman, at the mercy of a maelstrom of completely irrational emotions!

'Lord Dungarran!'

He turned. Hester was inside the room, still clutching the folder of papers, the family in a protective circle behind her. She looked red-eyed and thin, as if she had neither eaten nor slept for a week, and the drab, ink-stained garment she wore hung about her like a tent. The dress was short for her tall figure—it revealed ankles in wrinkled stockings and feet encased in clumsy boots, servants' boots. Her hair was dragged away from her face. With a sharp pang, he saw that the face itself had the inevitable smear of ink down one side.

And yet, on seeing her in the doorway his first thought had been that he had never seen anything so beautiful. Now, under the eyes of her family, it was a struggle to restrain himself from wiping the smear from her face and kissing her as he had kissed her, a century ago it seemed, in the little study in Grosvenor Street. Or would he first shake her till she cried for mercy, begged him for forgiveness for her heartless behaviour?

'Lord Dungarran?' Her manner was hesitant, as if she was unsure of what he would say.

Robert Dungarran hesitated. What *was* he to say? He was so fluent in society, so polished in address. What could he say to this girl? The feelings at war within were making it impossible for him to say anything. He looked at the papers still clutched in her hand. Their familiar look, the memory of the work Hester and he had toiled over for so long, loosened his tongue. Calmly—he must speak calmly—he said, 'Miss Perceval. You have the Pentacle papers there, I see.'

Her lips tightened. Surprise, then resentment showed in that tired face. 'Where else would they be?' she asked sharply.

Why hadn't she run to him, why hadn't she shown delight to see him, or regret that she had caused him such trouble! Anger won the battle for supremacy in Robert Dungarran's emotions. 'How the devil would I know where they would be, ma'am? With you, perhaps—but where was that? Vanished into thin air! Do you realise how much valuable time has been lost while you have been playing hide and seek, and I have been combing England for a trace of you?'

'Lord Dungarran—'

'Have you any idea of the confusion and distress you have caused with your silence?' he continued, sweeping aside her interruption. 'Look at your family! A few moments ago your mother was close to collapse. Her worry was short-lived, thank God, and is now at an end, but have you thought at all of Lady Martindale's feelings? I have never seen my aunt so distracted in her life—not even when my uncle died!'

'I am sorry for your aunt's distress, Lord Dungarran. Truly sorry. You will be able to reassure her when you return.' Hester's face was stony as she added, 'But instead of wasting valuable time berating me, you should be on your way to London. I have transcribed enough of the papers to know their secret. Lord Wellington's life is in danger. Some of the Spanish high command are in a plot to assassinate him.'

The news brought him up short. 'When? Where?'

'On the twentieth of next month—' She passed a hand over her forehead. 'Or is it this month? I have lost count of the days.'

Hugo said gently, 'Today is the third, Hester. The third of July.'

'Is it? The twentieth of this month, then—or very soon after. The Spaniards are due to meet Wellington for a conference on the road between Ciudad Rodrigo and Salamanca. The letters are not more precise than that.'

'They can't be—not with the uncertainty of the campaign. But they'll find him somewhere on that road. Our men must simply find him first. We have time—just! Hester, this is not the moment I know, but please forgive—'

'You should leave immediately, Lord Dungarran.' She put the folder down on the table with deliberation. 'There are the papers. Take them and finish them at your leisure. You needn't trouble to come back when you have delivered the message—I don't expect to see or hear from you again.'

'I must explain—'

'Don't try! I meant what I said. Goodbye. And—for Wellington's sake—God speed!'

Dungarran held out his hand, but she ignored it and with a quick look of apology at her family went out of the room. He was still staring at the door when Sir James spoke.

'Dungarran, I don't pretend to understand what has been going on,' he said with a troubled frown. 'But do you take what my daughter has said seriously?'

'Oh yes! It's perfectly serious—extremely serious, Sir James.'

'Then shouldn't you be going? I would invite you to eat something with us, but speed would seem to be essential. I'll get one of our people to put something up for your journey. Hugo, you might think of accompanying Lord Dungarran. If what Hester has told us is indeed true then we must make sure the message reaches the War Office safely and as soon as possible.'

'I shall leave immediately. Will you come, Hugo?'

'Of course! I'll get some things.' He went out. Dungarran turned to Sir James.

'There isn't time to explain why I behaved as I did a few moments ago. I…I was not myself. Could you perhaps talk to your daughter—persuade her to give me a chance to say how much I regret it?'

'I'll do my best, Dungarran.' The expression on Sir James's face was not reassuring. With a gesture of despair Dungarran picked up the folder of documents, turned on his heel and followed Hugo out.

After the two men had gone Hester wanted nothing more than to retreat from the world again. But her parents were hurt and angry at her deception of them. They could not understand why she and Lowell had kept her presence in Abbot Quincey such a secret. She owed them an account and an explanation. Lowell in fact did most of the telling, while she sat, her hand in that of her mother, listening and reliving the events of the past five days…

When Lowell had opened the door of the house in Half Moon Street Hester had such a shock that she burst into tears. 'Lowell! Oh, thank God you're still here!' she cried. 'I thought you had gone. Let me in— quickly!'

To his credit Lowell didn't ask questions there and then, but ushered her straight into the little salon. Here she sank into an armchair and tried to get her breath

back. But she leapt up again when she heard noises
outside in the street.

'The door! The door, Lowell! Is it shut fast? Tell
your man not to open it to anyone! Go, Lowell, go!'

'There's no one else here, Hes. And the door is
shut.'

'Bolt it, Lowell! Please!'

When Lowell returned he looked in concern at his
sister's pale, tear-stained cheeks and trembling limbs.
He pushed her back into the chair, then went in search
of brandy and glasses. When he came back he demanded, 'What on earth has happened, Hester? Is it
Dungarran? What has he done?'

'No, no, no! It's the Comte de Landres. He mustn't
find me!'

'De Landres? What the devil has de Landres to do
with you?' Hester tried to stammer out a few words,
but between fright and lack of breath she was inco-
herent.

In deep concern Lowell said gently, 'Hester, take
a sip of that drink, then calm down and tell me why
you're in such a state. Slowly now!'

Hester sipped the brandy, took a deep breath and
started an account of the morning's events. Before she
knew it, she was telling Lowell the whole story, beginning with the means Dungarran had used to black-
mail her into working with him…

'I should be shot, Hester! To give him such a hold
over you! But I would never have believed it of
Dungarran! I would have thought him incapable of
such ungentlemanly behaviour.'

'He…he would never have carried out his threat, Lowell. I realise that now. He is, truly, a gentleman. But let me tell you why he thought it so important for me to help him.' She went on to describe the days of patient decipherment, the feelings of triumph when they had found the key to the Pentacle papers… In the end Hester told him almost all of it, leaving out only Dungarran's kisses, and their astonishing effect on her. Such things were not relevant to her tale. But the rest of her story took a considerable time, for if Lowell was to help her he must know everything, including the newly discovered importance of the Pentacle papers. It was a relief to unburden herself to him. Lowell had been her confidant and accomplice for so many years, but the secret work she had been doing with Dungarran had recently put a wall between brother and sister. Now all was open again—except Dungarran's efforts to educate her in the tenderer arts. That was still private ground.

When she had finished, Lowell, who had been standing at the window, turned and asked, 'When did you say Dungarran will be back?'

'Not for forty-eight hours.'

'Hm.' Lowell finished his brandy. 'Well, I don't wish to worry you further, Hes, but there's a gent on the other side of the street who has been watching this house ever since he arrived five minutes ago. No! Don't come closer to the window! He's seen me, but he mustn't see you. Wait! He's coming over! Upstairs with you, and take your baggage with you!'

Hester waited round the bend at the top of the

stairs, heart beating so loudly that she thought their visitor must hear it.

'Mr Perceval? Mr Lowell Perceval?' The man's English accent was good, but not perfect.

'Sir?'

'Oh, excuse me, let me introduce myself! My name is Razan, Charles Razan. I am a friend of the Comte de Landres. May I come in?'

Hester heard footsteps entering the hall and going into the salon. Then Lowell's voice. 'May I know your business, sir?'

'Monsieur de Landres has charged me with a message for Miss Perceval. May I see her?'

Lowell's voice again, expressing polite bewilderment. 'My sister, sir? What makes you think she lives here?'

'Oh, I don't! But the servant at Lady Martindale's said he thought she might have come here to visit you.'

'Lady Martindale's servant was mistaken. Miss Perceval wouldn't even expect to find me here, I assure you. She thinks I'm out of London. And, except for a change in my plans, I would be. As it is, I shall be leaving very shortly, so I can't even offer to deliver a message if I see her. I'm sorry, but I can't help you.'

'Then I apologise for having disturbed you.' There was a pause. 'You are quite sure she isn't here?'

This time Lowell's voice was cold. 'Quite sure. I'll see you out. Good day, sir.' The door opened and was then shut and bolted. Lowell came up the stairs.

'You heard?'

Hester nodded. 'He wasn't convinced.'

'I'm not surprised. He saw the two brandy glasses. He'll be back—possibly with friends. I'm not sure what we should do.'

'Let's go to Abbot Quincey! The papers would be safe there. Lowell, let's go home! I can't think of anywhere in London where I could hide, and it's two days at least before Dungarran's return. I daren't go back to the house.'

'The Holyhead Mail leaves Wood Street at half past seven. We could catch that easily,' said Lowell thoughtfully. 'But what about Lady Martindale?'

'Heavens, yes! I hadn't thought! She'll be so worried when she comes back from Richmond! If I write a note for her can you get it delivered to Grosvenor Street?'

'I'll see to it. Say you're safe, but don't say where you are or what you're doing.'

'Why not?'

'Just in case the note falls into the wrong hands. I'll take you to the Cross Keys, leave you there to wait for the coach, then cut back to Grosvenor Street. If Lady Martindale is there I'll talk to her. If not, I'll leave the note with one of the servants. We'd better prepare to leave. Hester, I hope you'll be safe—de Landres and Razan won't be looking for you at the inn, will they?'

'They won't be looking for a young man. Are those clothes of Mr Gaines still here? Then fetch them and

I'll change. And I'd like a more suitable bag for these papers. But hurry!'

Lady Martindale had not yet returned when Lowell called, but she was expected at any moment. Though the house was in confusion, he was able to leave his note with one of the servants with strict instructions to deliver it the minute she arrived. He wasted no time for, as he later told her, he was not easy in his mind until he saw Hester safely waiting for him at the Cross Keys. No one would have recognised Miss Perceval in the young dandy sitting, one leg crossed over the other, quietly reading a newspaper in the corner. And Lowell was much reassured when she told him that, as far as she was aware, no one had shown any undue curiosity about the passengers for the Mail. They left on time, and the two Percevals, whose experience of such a mode of transport had till now been slight, spent an uncomfortable night as the coach rattled along until they reached Northampton in the early morning. Here they climbed out stiff and hungry, Hester still clutching her precious bag. They didn't stop for any refreshment. Lowell hired a couple of horses, and they set off for Abbot Quincey.

'I've been thinking, Lowell,' said Hester as they rode along the country lanes. 'It would be better if no one knew that I've come back.'

'Why not?'

'Mama would never let me work the way I need to if I am to decipher these papers in time, you know she wouldn't. And if de Landres or any of his henchmen should come to Perceval Hall, how long do you think it would be before they found out from Mama that I was here?'

Lowell nodded. 'But where could you hide? And where would you sleep?'

'In my attic. There's bound to be some sort of bed we could fetch in from one of the other attics. Food might be more of a problem…'

'I suppose I could bring you some, but if I came too often someone would be bound to ask what I was doing. And wouldn't you need clothes and someone to look after you?'

Hester thought for a moment. 'Could we ask Maggie to help? She wanders all over the place and no one ever takes any notice of her. She'd manage the clothes, and I should think she could manage the food, too.' Hester was tired and suffering from reaction, but she managed an affectionate smile. 'Think of the way she managed us when we were children! I'm sure she'd do it—especially if *you* asked her, Lowell! You were always her baby, her favourite. Maggie would never say no to you!'

So they decided that Lowell would help Hester up to the attics by an unused staircase at the back of the house, and then go to find Maggie. They would have to improvise from then on. Whatever happened, Hester was determined to work without interruption until she had finally found out the secret of the Pentacle papers. When Lowell asked her she told him why.

'Those papers have become a…a sort of challenge.

To me personally. I'm not particularly proud of deceiving Mama and Papa, or of playing a part with Dungarran in front of society. I took the papers in order to save them, and if I can find out their message then I shall feel the things I've done have been justified.'

'I thought you might have been doing this for Dungarran…?'

'Of course not!' Lowell raised an eyebrow at her, and Hester pulled a face and went on, 'Well, in a way I am. I want to show him. I want to prove to him that I'm a force to be reckoned with, not just a…' She glanced at Lowell. 'Well you know as well as I do that Dungarran is a…a…' She tried again. 'He enjoys what he calls 'light dalliance', and I want him to take me seriously.'

'You're in love with him!'

'That's nonsense! Absolute rubbish! You're an idiot, Lowell! I didn't mean as a woman—I meant take me seriously in my work!' Lowell looked at her speculatively as they rode on. It seemed to him that his sister was protesting just a little too much, but he decided not to pursue the subject. Hester had enough to worry about.

They reached the stables behind Perceval Hall before the household was stirring. By this time Hester was near to collapse, but Lowell was always at his best when facing a challenge. In no time, Hester found herself in her attic, sitting in her favourite armchair while Lowell set about rearranging the furniture.

'Bear up, Hes! Don't give in now! We'll soon have

you settled.' He cast a satisfied glance round the room. 'There! There's space for a bed in here, and Maggie will know where I can find one. I'll go now to fetch her—I won't be long.' He came back and hugged her. 'Don't look like that, Hes! A few hours sleep and you'll be as good as new.'

Lowell soon returned with their old nurse. Maggie might grumble, but she was too soft-hearted to refuse her favourite. Sworn to secrecy, she fetched sheets and pillows from the linen cupboard, while Lowell dragged a truckle bed from a neighbouring attic. Hester hardly heard her scolding, barely felt Maggie's work-roughened hands gently exchanging Woodford Gaines's clothes for a cotton wrap. Before she realised it she found herself tucked up in bed between cool, lavender-scented sheets in her own, dear, familiar refuge. The last thing she saw before falling asleep was the bag of papers on the floor beside the bed.

Chapter Twelve

She slept for several hours, then woke with a start. Maggie was putting a cup of chocolate and some rolls beside the bed. Then she disappeared again. Hester was so hungry that, by the time Maggie returned carrying a basin and ewer, the food was all gone. 'I'll fetch some clothes for you as soon as I can,' she said, looking disapprovingly at Woodford Gaines's clothing, now somewhat the worse for wear. 'You canna wear those garments, Miss Hester. It isn't fit.'

'It isn't important what I wear, Maggie. No one will see me but you and Master Lowell. But I must start on those papers straight away.'

Maggie sniffed. 'I'll fetch the things your mother left for the village. There'll be something there that'll fit you.' A few minutes later she was back with some undergarments and a rough, brown cotton dress. Hester, still in her wrapper, was already laying the Pentacle papers out on her desk and arranging her pens. Within minutes she was hard at work, her hair screwed back out of the way, and the drab dress already christened with ink.

About halfway through the morning Lowell appeared to see how she was. He laughed at her absorption, but seemed comforted by it.

'No need to worry about you, that's obvious.'

'What did the family say when you came back so unexpectedly?'

'They exclaimed, of course, and asked what I was doing here. I told them I'd been planning a trip to Devon, but it had been called off at the last minute—which is perfectly true! I forgot to tell you yesterday—Gaines's godfather has been taken ill. That's why I was still in London. To say the truth, the family are all so busy with the Steepwood business that they hardly noticed I was there! What a mess it is, Hester! However, Pa and the others seem to be managing, though the neighbourhood won't really settle down until we all know who the new owner is. What about you? Do you need anything else?'

'I shall need more pens. These wear out so fast, and I haven't time to mend them.'

'Give them to me. I'm a dab hand at mending pens.'

Over the next few days, with Lowell to give her the necessary support and Maggie to look after her physical needs, Hester devoted all her attention and energy to the business of deciphering the Pentacle papers. Buried in the long, elaborate phrases of Spanish diplomatic language, accompanied with terse French comments, a picture was emerging of a tiny group of dissident Spaniards. They had no cause to love the French—Napoleon had invaded their country, taken over Madrid, their capital, and installed his brother Joseph there as their upstart king. Yet these

Spanish grandees were in secret correspondence with French agents. Their letters expressed their burning resentment of the British command in the Spanish Peninsula—in particular, the high-handed manner in which all strategic decisions were taken without reference to some of the noblest, the greatest, the most talented generals in Spain. The flames of their anger had been fanned by skilful handling on the part of the French, and matters had reached a point where one or two of the Spaniards were ready to take action. Assassination was mentioned. But whose? The Spaniards were still too cautious to mention names. Hester toiled on, barely taking time for sleep or food. She had saved the Pentacle papers from destruction. But in bringing them to Abbot Quincey she had also taken on a heavy responsibility. Someone's life— probably that of Lord Wellington—was in danger. She must not rest until she knew it all.

And eventually, after working till she was in danger of dropping, she had it. She had just finished writing the summary of everything she had learned when Lowell came bursting into the attic with the news that Dungarran was in the hall asking to see her father.

Lost in her own reliving of the story, Hester had barely been aware of Lowell's voice, her parents' questions and his replies. Now she roused herself. Lowell had brought them up to the moment when she had appeared in the doorway. She turned to her mother.

'Mama... I'm sorry! Indeed I am! I didn't think of anything but the papers. It wasn't until I saw your

face…and…and Dungarran spoke… Forgive me…'
Her voice choked.

Lady Perceval put her arms round her daughter. 'Of
course you're forgiven!' she said. 'Your Papa and I
are proud of you, Hester. But now you must go to
bed. You need rest. We'll talk of all this later, when
you aren't quite so exhausted. Come!'

Sir James kissed his daughter on her way out. 'I
suppose I must forgive you, too, though I still think
you could have told us. But Dungarran was very
harsh. It's all up to him and Hugo now. I wonder how
they're faring?'

After telling her story Hester found it impossible
to stay awake. She fell into an exhausted slumber
which lasted almost forty-eight hours, broken only for
a sip of water or some of the soup brought by her
mother or one of the maids. Waking or sleeping, she
had no thought for anything outside her bedchamber
walls—London, Lady Martindale, the Pentacle papers, Wellington himself, might never have existed.
Even Robert Dungarran. But this respite did not last.
After two days she was restored to full activity and
consciousness, and…misery.

The day had still been young when Hugo and
Dungarran had set out, and they travelled as speedily
as the post horses would take them. They were in
London by early evening. Dungarran took a few
minutes to inform his aunt that Hester had been
found, then hurried on to the Horse Guards. Here he
was lucky enough to catch one of Lord Bathurst's
most able lieutenants. The situation was quickly ex-
plained and as quickly understood. In no time two of

the army's best men had been despatched to Lisbon with the message, and four others had been called in and given instructions. Two of them would take a different sea route to Corunna, and make their separate ways through Northern Spain with the aid of the Spanish guerrillas. The last two would be smuggled in at Calais, and travel the more dangerous land route, using ways known only to themselves through the hostile territory of France. The message was sure to reach Wellington by one means or another.

Robert Dungarran took Hugo back to his aunt's house. Over dinner Lady Martindale and Hugo talked. Robert was markedly silent.

'I am not at all surprised you're tired and out of sorts, Robert,' said Lady Martindale. 'You've been chasing about the country without stopping for days! You've earned a long rest.'

'Thank you. I suppose I shall take one,' her nephew answered shortly.

Hugo exchanged a look with Lady Martindale. 'Why don't you come back with me?' he asked. 'I'd enjoy your company, now that things seem to have settled down on the estate.' He grinned. 'You could come to our fête on the eighteenth. Now, you would enjoy that!'

His friend looked at him sourly. 'I don't know why you always think of me as a town-lover, Hugo, indeed I don't! Have you forgotten the Dungarran lands in Hertfordshire? And the house in the Cotswolds—not to mention the Irish estates, and the hunting lodge in Leicestershire? I am well used to country pursuits and duties, believe me.'

'Then you won't mind coming to our fête!' Hugo turned to his hostess. 'What about you, Lady Martindale? Would you like a sojourn in the country? London society must be getting rather flat now. You were very kind to Hester. My parents would welcome you.'

'I hardly think so, Hugo! What? Welcome the woman who lost their only daughter for more than four days?'

'The circumstances were…a little unusual. Part of the blame lies with Hester, surely? And she is now quite safely restored to them. No, I'm sure they have forgotten. I think you should both come.'

'I am certain your sister would like to see Aunt Martindale. But she would refuse to see me.' Dungarran got up from the table and went over to the fireplace. 'I was unforgivably rude to her this morning.'

'You, Robert? Rude? Unforgivably rude? I don't believe it!'

'I was in a rage. Hugo was there. He'll tell you.'

Lady Martindale looked astonished. 'Can this be true, Hugo?'

'Yes. In fact, Robert was deuced unfair to Hester. I asked him about it on the journey down, but he wouldn't explain. I've never seen him like it before. In fact—' Hugo hesitated. 'In fact, if it wasn't Robert we were talking about, I'd think he was…'

Lady Martindale leaned forward. 'Yes?'

'I'd think he was…in…'

'In love?'

'Ridiculous, isn't it?'

'Of course it is!' Robert Dungarran said bitterly.

'Go on, laugh, both of you. Thirty-one years old and I've fallen in love for the first time. Ridiculously in love. I've lost my head, my reason, my self-respect, and this morning I lost my temper. Your sister, Hugo, has never shown a liking for marriage, and not much for me, but now she will never be persuaded to consider either. Very amusing!'

'Robert! Dearest! I never thought to see this day! Oh, I'm so happy for you.'

'Happy for me? My dear aunt, are you mad? Did you not hear? Hester Perceval will refuse even to meet me. She will never let herself love me.'

'Unless I am very much mistaken, she already does.'

'Lady Martindale, Robert is right.' Hugo's face was troubled. 'Hester has always sworn she would never marry. You may be right about her sentiments, but she can be remarkably pig-headed when she chooses.'

'As we all know,' said Robert Dungarran.

'I am ashamed of you! If a personable gentleman, with everything to recommend him, cannot persuade a young lady, who is more than half in love with him already, to marry him, then I shall... I shall eat my best hat! Mind you, I am not saying it will be easy, but that is not at all a bad thing. You've always found too much favour with the ladies.'

'So you have told me, Godmama. I am pleased that one of us can be happy.'

Lady Martindale smiled at Hugo. 'Hugo, I don't think it wise in the circumstances to accept your parents' hospitality. But I think cousins of my late husband live somewhere in the neighbourhood, and we shall wheedle an invitation out of them. I look forward to seeing Hester and your parents again, and would love to come to your fête! Robert must please himself.'

Lady Martindale wasted no time. She managed to catch her relatives just before they left London for the country, and received an enthusiastic invitation. Within a day or two she and her nephew joined them at Courtney Hall, just five miles from Abbot Quincey.

Hugo had preceded them to Northamptonshire, anxious to assure his sister that Wellington's life was secure. It was the only part of his news which pleased her. The rest—that Lady Martindale and Robert Dungarran were only five miles away, that Dungarran intended to call again very soon—was enough to send her back up to her attic, like a wounded animal seeking a hiding place. But the attic, which had been such a refuge in the past, held little consolation. She sat huddled in her armchair for hours, using all her powers of reason, all the intelligence she had so prided herself on, to cure the ache in her heart. She had been perfectly right to dismiss Dungarran as she had. Why on earth should she waste another moment's thought on him? He was an ingrate, a cold-hearted opportunist, who used people for his own ends, ignoring the fact that they were living, feeling human beings. She had overcome her panic to rescue his papers for him, gone through so much anxiety until she had found Lowell, she had undertaken a hideously uncomfortable overnight journey to Abbot Quincey, deceived her family, starved and gone without sleep to finish the transcription... And what were his first words? Not that he was glad to see her, not that he was amazed at what she had done for him. She hadn't existed. His concern was for the papers. *'Miss Perceval. You have the Pentacle papers there, I see!'* He was a man without a heart and she would have no more to do with him. A feeling of desolation overcame her. Zeno would have to go, too. What was she to do now that her friendship with him was over? How would she fill her days?

'Hester! Hester!' Lowell's voice. She pulled herself together and got up. Lowell came bursting into the room. 'Dungarran's here and Mama wants you!'

'Please tell Mama that I'll come down in a little while. When Lord Dungarran has gone.'

'I can't do that,' said Lowell, shocked. 'She was very insistent. I think Dungarran has come to see Papa. You'd better come down, Hes.'

Hester followed Lowell down the stairs and into the main body of the house. As soon as she was visible her mother caught her by the arm and dragged her along into her bedchamber. 'My dear, clever girl, what a conquest! You must change, Hester! Your maid has laid out a dress for you, and she's waiting to do your hair.' She was bustled into her room, where the maid started her ministrations.

'Mama, why the fuss? I don't intend to meet…anyone.'

'Yes, you will, Hester! I insist! And so does your Papa!'

Hester grew pale. 'I assume you mean me to see Lord Dungarran. Mama, you can't be so unkind!'

'Unkind? Unkind?' Lady Perceval was outraged. 'Allow me to tell you, Hester Perceval, that not many young ladies are given the chance to marry into one of the richest families in England!'

'Marry! Do you mean to say that that…that man has the effrontery to come here with a proposal of marriage?'

'What are you saying? Effrontery? Really, Hester, I sometimes wonder whether your studies have turned your brain! Robert Dungarran comes from an old and respected family, he is rich, charming and altogether extremely eligible. A matrimonial prize of the first degree, and a very elusive one! It is a most flattering offer! Now let me hear no more nonsense! You will receive Dungarran, and you will listen to what he has to say!'

Lady Perceval was not to be swayed and Hester resigned herself to facing the man she had sworn to avoid, and, if her mother was right, to listen to a proposal of marriage she was determined to refuse. She received him in the small parlour.

'Lord Dungarran,' she said coldly, as she curtseyed.

'Miss Perceval, I…I have your father's permission to…' He stopped, then said abruptly, 'Would you take a walk in the grounds with me? It's a fine day, and this room brings to mind a scene I would rather forget.'

Hester made no move. 'Why should that be? It was surely the scene of one of your greatest successes— the secret of the Pentacle papers delivered to you in time to be effective. And, by someone who, being a woman, would hardly expect any acknowledgement, any respect or admiration for work involving the mind competently done. It was quite astounding that I was trusted with it in the first place.'

'That is rubbish, and you know it! Give me ten minutes in the privacy and peace of the grounds and I can show you how highly I regard you, how much I acknowledge the superiority of your gifts. And how very much I love you and hope you will marry me.'

'Very flatteringly put. But too late. I do not need ten minutes anywhere to remind you, Lord Dungarran, that I have never had the slightest intention of marrying anyone. And after our closer acquaintance I can now assure you that, if I ever did change my mind, it would not be in favour of you!' Hester could hear her voice rising angrily on these last words and stopped. This was not the behaviour recommended by books on deportment for young ladies receiving a proposal of marriage. She took a breath and said sweetly and falsely, 'I am sorry if this causes you pain, but—'

But Robert Dungarran, fortified by a short, informative chat with Lowell on the way in, said with a wry grin, 'I doubt that! I doubt that very much indeed. And if it gives you any satisfaction, yes, you are causing me pain. But I refuse to depart as I no doubt should, with a manly smile and protestations of undying, if hopeless, regard! I am convinced that we could find happiness together in spite of your obstinate insistence—'

'The arrogance of men! I've heard enough! It's time you went, sir!'

'I'll go for now—it's obvious you won't listen to me today. But I'm not giving up, Hester. It's too important to me.' He came up to her and, taking a firm hold of her hands, looked deep into her eyes. 'Have you any idea how rare this is—this harmony of mind and body that flows between us? No, don't argue! Harmony, Hester! Think of the hours we spent working together—can you deny the instinctive understanding between us? And as for the body... I can remind you of the sweetest harmony of all...' He bent his head and though Hester pulled frantically away from him he refused to let her go. He trapped her in his arms and gave her a gentle kiss. But gentle or passionate—it made little difference. Her treacherous body melted as soon as their lips met...

'No!' she cried, and tore herself out of his arms. 'No! I won't be seduced into marriage by—what did you call them?—''the pleasures of light dalliance''. I won't be your wife! I refuse to be any man's chattel or slave! And you may come here as often as you choose, Lord Dungarran—I shall not see you! Whatever my parents might say!'

His face was stern as he said, 'Chattel? Slave? You demean yourself, and me, by such talk! This is no light dalliance, Hester! I want you for my companion, my partner, and I offer you a home, and children...and a lifetime's devotion. I won't let you cast them aside. Not without a fight. Be warned.' He turned on his heel and went out.

Hester ran to the window and watched him striding away from the house towards the stables. He had always seemed tall, but here in the country he looked broader, more powerful. It was easier to believe that he was as gifted an athlete as Hugo. She turned away. This morning she had caught a glimpse of a new Robert Dungarran. The elegant man of the London drawing-rooms, with his air of detachment, his drawl and his lazy manner had been replaced with something more disturbing. His last words had revealed an aspect of his character which was, she was sure, known to very few. He had spoken seriously, almost severely, with a sense of deep sincerity. Was this the real Robert Dungarran? In speaking slightingly of herself as his wife she had offended him. Why? Was it because he really did have a view of marriage which demanded equal respect and support between man and wife? If so, it was an ideal which was radically different from her own jaundiced view. Which of them was nearer the reality?

Hester sought the isolation of her attic while she debated these questions. She considered her parents' marriage. Her mother did not pretend to be clever, but her father treated her with respect and love, and recent events proved what a support they were to each other. Among her own generation Beatrice Roade's marriage was full of love and humour, and what an asset Harry had been to her in dealing with her somewhat difficult father! Others came to mind, perhaps not so obviously ideal, but the couples involved seemed to be satisfied. Had she been over-influenced by her education at Mrs Guarding's? Had her first experience of London prejudiced her for life? And was she cutting herself off from something which could be…wonderful?

She resolutely refused to come down when Dungarran called. He had weapons to persuade her, which she was sure he would not scruple to use, and she wanted to think things out for herself. Each time he came he left a note for her with Lowell. They were all in cipher, which was as well, for some of them were not the sort she would have wished her mother to see. They all contained the wit and humour which she had associated with Zeno, and, though perhaps she did not realise it, they were, in their way, as disarming as his physical presence. But then one came which sent her raging out into the grounds like an avenging fury.

She found the note, as usual, on her desk, and, as usual, set about transcribing it. But before she was halfway through her cheeks were scarlet. It was one of the more lurid passages from *The Wicked Marquis*. Attached to it was a message. It ran: 'Only three people in the world know the author's name, though many more would like to. Shall we tell them? Or would you like to discuss the matter first? Two o'clock this afternoon by the big cedar.' No signature—but none was necessary.

She stormed out of the house and over the lawns at ten past two that afternoon ready for battle.

'You're early! That's good.' He gave her one of his smiles, the dangerous sort, the sort to charm an unwary bird out of a tree.

Hester stopped in her tracks. The smile was doing things to her, she had never felt more like an unwary bird. She pulled herself together. 'You said two o'clock!'

'I expected you to keep me waiting at least half an hour. Shall we walk on?' When Hester hesitated he added, 'It's perfectly proper. Your mother knows you're in the grounds with me. She trusts me.'

'She doesn't know any better,' said Hester bitterly. 'She thinks you're a gentleman, not a blackmailer.'

She fell into step with him and they walked towards the bridge by the lake.

'I had to do something, my love. You were never going to give me a chance to explain otherwise.'

'I'm not your love!'

'Oh, you are! Whatever you might say or do, you will be my love. For ever. Don't ask me to explain that, Hester, because I can't. And that reminds me…' He took a parcel out of the pocket of his coat. 'I must give you this.'

She unwrapped it and looked up at him in surprise. 'My apron! My blue apron.'

'I found it on the floor of the study after you had disappeared. From that moment on I was hardly rational.' He gave her a whimsical smile. 'Absurd, isn't it? Robert Dungarran, the advocate of logic, Zeno, the mathematician and believer in the supreme power of reason, both turned upside down by a girl in a blue apron with ink on her face! That's what happened, Hester. I fell in love with you in this blue apron, though I didn't realise it till much later. And when the truth did hit me I had no idea how to deal with it! You stood in that doorway, surrounded by your family, and I didn't know whether I wanted to kiss you, beat you or ravish you on the spot. A fine, mixed-up state for Robert Dungarran to be in—especially as not one of them was possible! So I went back to what I did know, what we had chiefly shared—the Pentacle papers. I knew it was the wrong thing to say. But I couldn't for the life of me think of anything else! I was paralysed.'

'I was so hurt! When Lowell told me you had arrived I could hardly stand on my feet, but I wanted to see you… And then…and then…'

'You believed my only thought was for the papers. Hester, I swear to you that when I saw you my head, my heart—everything I am—was full of you. Mentioning the papers was merely a…a line of communication when everything else was so confused that I didn't know where to begin.'

'You were angry.'

'I was furious! Try to understand what it was like, Hester. I can't remember a time when I was not in control of my feelings—my aunt would tell you that I was always too detached, never cared enough. Mathematics was my passion, and formulae and equations are not likely to arouse violent emotion. I had always shunned irrational attachments, even despised them. But you had taken possession of my heart before I knew it!'

Hester was in a state of agitation, her restless hands twisting the apron into an unrecognisable rag. Robert Dungarran gently removed it. 'I'll hold this for you, Hester. I don't want it lost.'

'You say your world has been turned upside down,' she cried. 'But so has mine! Ever since I was seventeen I have known what I would do with my future. Marriage played no part in it. And now…and now… You have come along again with your smiles, and your wit, and your looks…and…the rest—'

'My kisses?'

'Yes, damn you, your kisses! And I no longer know what I wish for…' Tears started to trickle down Hester's face. 'How do I know what marriage to you

would be like? How do I know whether we should
be happy?'

He took her chin and lifted her eyes to his. 'You
can't,' he said gravely. 'Some things have to be taken
on trust. But would you be any happier without me?'
She was silenced. He took out his handkerchief and
wiped her face. 'At least it isn't ink,' he said with a
faint smile.

Hester turned away, still silent.

'Hester, you've now heard what I had to say. I
cannot imagine life without you. But you are clearly
not yet convinced. May I make a suggestion?' He saw
that she was listening. 'May we meet tomorrow—and
every day after that—until you are certain of what
you want? Let me try to persuade you that we have
the best possible chance of happiness together. And
if you are still not convinced…' Hester looked at him.
His smile was twisted. 'I shall not bother you after
that.'

For the next few days Hester met Robert Dungarran
in the grounds every day. Every day she learned more
about him—his quirky sense of humour, his consideration, his deep love of the countryside—aspects of
his character which had never appeared during their
acquaintance in London. Together they helped with
preparations for the fête which was imminent, and she
saw how easy he was with a wide variety of people—
her family, visitors, tradesmen, servants, farmers.

Every morning he sent her a love letter—love letters which must be unique, for they were all in complicated ciphers which she had to work hard to solve.
Some sentences made her laugh, some moved her be-

yond measure, and parts of them brought a vivid blush to her cheeks. At the end of a week Robert Dungarran had succeeded. Hester Perceval, one-time dedicated spinster, had so changed that she was seriously contemplating marriage. But how was she to tell the man of her choice?

The day of the fête dawned bright and sunny. The whole family was thrown into a welter of last-minute preparation, followed by appearances during the fête itself. This was a huge success, the only mishap being the collapse of an awning over Hugo's head, just when he was about to present the prize pig. No damage was done except perhaps to Hugo's dignity, and much innocent fun was had in the attempts to retrieve the pig. But eventually the crowds had gone, the servants were beginning the work of clearing up and Hester could wait no longer. She sought out Robert Dungarran.

'We…we haven't had our walk today,' she said nervously.

'Would you like one now?' he said instantly. 'I think we have both done enough for Abbot Quincey and its fête, don't you? Come! Let's walk through the woods.'

The sun was still hot enough to make the shade of the trees very welcome. By now they were usually at ease in each other's company, but today the mood was different. The bright flashes of sunshine, glinting and dancing through the leaves, enhanced the atmosphere of bright expectation. They stopped.

'Well, Hester?'

'I…er…I…' She took a deep breath and began

again. 'Your note this morning… The cipher was
harder than usual. I…I didn't manage all of it.'

'Dear me—didn't you?'

'Er…no. This bit…' She took out a piece of paper
and showed it to him. 'Wh…what does it mean?'

He looked at her with a gleam in his eye. 'Shall I
show you?'

'Er…yes. Please.'

Robert Dungarran took her in his arms and kissed
her, sweetly and gently. 'Was that it?'

'N…not all of it. There's more.' And she pointed
to the following paragraph.

'That? I wouldn't have thought that difficult. Let
me see… How do I begin?' His hold grew tighter and
this time his kiss lasted until Hester was trembling in
his grasp. Her arms crept round his neck and she returned the kiss with fervour. The passion between
them slowly mounted, their bodies melting into each
other in the dancing leaping light surrounding them…

'*Hester!*' Robert Dungarran raised his head and
held her away until the white hot feeling running between them gradually cooled. He considered her for
a moment.

'Unless you are an unprincipled wanton, my sweet
love, you've just made a declaration.'

Hester held shaking hands to her cheeks. 'I…I
didn't know how to bring the subject up,' she said.
'And you have recently been so discreet…'

'Discreet! If you knew the restraint I've had to put
on myself… So you knew what was in my note all
the time?'

'Most of it, yes. There's a piece at the end…'

'Ah, yes! The last paragraph. That was quite deliberately hard. And it defeated you!' His smile was complacent.

'I could have done it if I'd had more time!' cried Hester, jealous of her reputation. 'But with the fête…'

'How sad! Time is not what you're going to get.'

'Oh! Then will you tell me? Or…' she smiled invitingly. 'Show me?'

'I'll tell you, if you do something first. Showing will come afterwards.'

'After what?'

'First,' he said, taking her in his arms again, 'you have to kiss me and promise to marry me.'

Hester put her arms up and brought his head down to hers. This kiss was different again from all the rest. It was long, sweet, and serious, a solemn dedication. 'I'll marry you, Robert, and do my best to be what you want me to be.'

'My dear love!' He lifted her into the air, laughing with triumphant joy, and then brought her slowly down again to his lips.

'And now will you show me?'

'No, my darling Hester. Not now. That comes later. After we are married.'

'Tell me then!'

He bent his head and spoke softly in her ear. Hester's eyes grew round and her cheeks grew rosy. 'Robert!' she said. 'Is that really so? Then…how soon can we be married?'

Modern Romance™
...seduction and
passion guaranteed

Tender Romance™
...love affairs that
last a lifetime

Sensual Romance™
...sassy, sexy and
seductive

Sizzling Romance™
...sultry days and
steamy nights

Medical Romance™
...medical drama on
the pulse

Historical Romance™
...rich, vivid and
passionate

29 new titles every month.

With all kinds of Romance for
every kind of mood...

MILLS & BOON®

Makes any time special™

MAT3

READER SERVICE™

The best romantic fiction direct to your door

Our guarantee to you...

*The Reader Service involves you in no obligation
to purchase, and is truly a service to you!*

*There are many extra benefits including a free
monthly Newsletter with author interviews,
book previews and much more.*

*Your books are sent direct to your door
on 14 days no obligation home approval.*

*We offer huge discounts on selected books
exclusively for subscribers.*

*Plus, we have a dedicated Customer Care team
on hand to answer all your queries on
(UK) 020 8288 2888
(Ireland) 01 278 2062.*

GEN/GU/1

Medical Romance™
6 brand new titles each month
...medical drama
on the pulse.
Available on subscription every month
from the Reader Service™
GEN/03/RS2